Timecrunch

The Trails of Death

LEON G. CAESAR

For book orders, email orders@traffordpublishing.com.sg

Most Trafford Singapore titles are also available at major online book retailers.

Printed in Singapore.

ISBN: 978-1-4907-0194-3 (sc)
ISBN: 978-1-4907-0195-0 (hc)
ISBN: 978-1-4907-0196-7 (e)

Trafford rev. 11/29/2013

Trafford   www.traffordpublishing.com.sg

Singapore
toll-free: 800 101 2656 (Singapore)
Fax: 800 101 2656 (Singapore)

This book is devoted to my lovely daughters,
Nicole, Nadia and Chanté.
No amount of words can describe
how much I love and adore them.

In honour of my mother, Dorothy Pauline Caesar.

ACKNOWLEDGEMENTS

This novel would have taken much longer to complete had it not been for the interest and support of my good friend, Clarrissa Swain.

My heartfelt thanks to my sisters, Tesna Clarke and Norma Caesar as well as my daughters, Nicole, Nadia and Chanté for their continuous encouragement. My son, Hadley Bosman, unbeknowingly gave me many ideas to work with.

Misha Geidt and Alfred Mthimkhulu made valuable comments when the manuscript was still in its infant stage.

Thanks to Noeleen Corrigan Barazi, who went through the manuscript with a fine comb. But the responsibility for any mistakes remains mine and mine alone.

Finally (and I deliberately saved this for last) I am indebted to my wife, Grace Bosman Caesar, whose love has made me a better man and writer.

ACKNOWLEDGMENTS

PART ONE
WOE AND WONDER

CHAPTER 1

---◆━━◆◦❍◦❍◦◆◦❍◦━━◆---

Time Bubbled

G erry gazes lazily at the sea of faces around him. The delegates are literally from the four corners of the world, gathering in the Great Assembly Hall which houses fifty thousand people comfortably. Almost every seat is occupied. The atmosphere is thick and palpable. He searches amongst the expanse of faces . . . What are they thinking? Every now and then, he nods acknowledgement. The hall is exceptionally quiet for such a huge event, with only a few people speaking in hushed tones. He reads excitement and anticipation in every frown, twitch and fidget, and hears it in every breath and sigh.

It is a struggle to contain all the emotions welled up inside him; he focuses his restless eyes on the stage, which is situated in the front of the majestic hall. Lenny is at the centre of the stage, sitting in a chair next to a lectern. He is the only person on the giant stage, with Jodi standing on the other side of the reading desk—which is a little to Lenny's left—waiting for instructions.

At the back of the stage is the gigantic media screen, which issues from a small globe-like crystal attached at the bottom of the wall. The screen gives the appearance of solidity, though it is, in fact, insubstantial, as it is created by a combination of photons and quarks that are emitted by the crystal. The media screen almost covers the breadth of the stage—except for the space taken up by the control room, which is at the very edge of the stage to Lenny's left and reaches almost to the ceiling. In front of Lenny and Jodi, on a table—or rather, elevated about ten centimetres above it, like a gloomy epergne—is the object that wields the power that brought this multitude of faces together.

It is rather small and Gerry cannot see it clearly; he looks at the small media screen in the back of the seat in front of him and studies the object, looking for clues.

Suddenly the hushed tones change into a pregnant silence that hovers overhead like a bloated bubble trying not to burst, as the elderly, but firm, grey man rises from his seat and moves to the front of the stage, seemingly not in any hurry. *The old codger is dragging out the suspense,* Gerry thinks with a smile. A disappointing clamour bursts the nervous silence as Lenny pretends to go back to his seat.

He laughs so heartily that he infects the entire assembly.

Built-in microphones fill the massive space with his soft, sonorous, velvety voice.

"Forgive me, friends, I could not help myself. I wish you could see your faces! The Great Assembly Hall has never been home to so much anxiety!" He waits for the laughter to die down. "My fellow assemblers, after that impromptu exordium, now to the business at hand. It is an absolute honour to be standing in front of you, on this day and on this special occasion. To all the viewers of this event, I greet you too in the name of the Council of the Realm, on whose behalf I am officiating. But let me first tell you about my friend. What do you think of Gerry? At the council meeting where this assembly was planned, he said to me in all seriousness, 'Lenny, I think you should lead the assembly because you are the oldest person alive in the whole world today, and, you know, you are the only person on your fourth set of teeth'. Now, the age thing I can still understand, but what does my teeth have to do with the assembly—am I supposed to bite the time capsule—or take a bite out of time itself? The bugger, but I have news for him—these old bones can still rumba the socks off a quinquagenarian like him!" He makes a quick duple step, then suddenly grabs his back in a feign of agony.

He has his audience in stitches. Yeah, Lenny can be as mad as a hatter when he has his moments.

"I think I have to show you my entrechat some other time."

The laughter goes on quite long, then stops suddenly as if everyone remembers why he or she is here.

"This he said after the Science Academy informed the council of the inscription on the metal box—which reads: Time Capsule 2012-08-15. Needless to say, he managed to persuade the council that I should facilitate the assembly, which, do not get me wrong, is a great honour indeed."

As he utters these words, the stage screen comes alive and the inscription appears on it, on the screens at the back of each seat, as well as on all the media screens around the world—wherever people are tuned in.

A state of silent captivation suddenly descends on the assembly.

"Yes, I know some of you already worked it out—the box was buried 7254 years ago! Our amazing science community struggled for an entire month to make out the rusted and eaten-away inscription that was no longer clear to the naked eye or to any existing equipment. They had to invent a new instrument and a new chemical process for the purpose! Let us applaud their great efforts."

He continues after the clapping subsides, "Before we open the capsule, I have the privilege to introduce to you the man who found it during a construction operation—Gaston Margolis! Gaston, smile into your media screen please . . ."

The smiling face of a mature-looking young man, clean-shaven, with piercing, clear eyes, looms on all the screens. He grins, waves, and says, "Good afternoon, all."

"Thank you, Gaston, and thank you for your watchfulness. Now, at last, it is time to do what you have all been delegated to experience here today—let's open the box! But first, let me say this: the box has not been opened, but it was x-rayed to confirm that it contains no harmful substances. Now, let us get on with it! I introduce to you, Jodi, who, with Zedon—who is in the control room at the moment—represents Council Control. Jodi will open the box for us." Zedon, of middle-aged appearance—dressed in a semi-formal pants and jumper—comes out of the room, bows and goes back.

Jodi, dressed in a pretty avocado-green blouse and narrow-sleeved trousers, looks like a stunningly beautiful woman, with medium-length flowing black hair, slightly upward-slanted green eyes, high cheekbones and full, luscious cherry lips. She walks over to the elevated box with an exuberant cheer and clap from the audience. She bows her lithe and slender body and says, "It is my privilege." She flashes a broad and sparkling smile with her perfect teeth.

Silence again as all eyes follow her every athletic movement. She comes up to the box and gives it a preparative scan with eyes that can see through almost anything. She then grips the box in the palm of her left hand and, with her right, she pulls off the locking mechanism and the lid opens ever so slowly, with a woeful clang. She scours the contents with her extraordinary eyes, causing the image of everything she sees to be broadcast all over the world.

Everyone in the hall quickly presses and pulls on the screens in front of him or her to highlight angles of certain images and save their preferences.

"I confirm that the box contains no danger." With that, she hands something brownish to Lenny, whose face is now total concentration.

"Looks like a stained sheet of something in a wrapping. Jodi, your analysis please."

"It is a sheet of processed wood pulp called paper—used thousands of years ago—discoloured by age, a letter, fairly well preserved because it has been sealed in a vacuum bag made of a primitive substance called plastic. I recommend that you do not open the bag unless the contents of the letter are secured. I am now sending the contents to control for capturing . . . Next . . ." Her equanimity belies the crescendo of excitement that has taken hold of the very building.

"Very well then, thanks, my friends," Lenny breaks the silence. "Let us first take out and identify everything."

Gerry hears the pounding of his heart behind his ears, the slow breathing all around him. Across the world, more than ninety percent of the population is mesmerised in front of all sorts of media screens; not a soul can be found ambulating outside.

"Lock of hair of Melanie Adam," Jodi announces in her honey-sweet voice as she reads the label on the next packet; she hands it to Lenny, who puts it on the table, the label facing him.

"Lock of hair of Madeleine Adam."

"Lock of hair of Brumin Adam—my sensors tell me there are some foreign human hairs mixed with his."

"Lock of hair of Pablo Adam."

"Brumin's television game, musical compact disk of Madeleine, recording of Melanie's favourite television programme and my cigar . . . I have been reading the labels . . . That is the lot, Lenny." He arranges everything neatly on the table.

Amazing, thinks Gerry. *The time capsule has certainly brought forth a dramatic array of effects.* He tries to figure out just why anyone would put tresses in a time capsule, when Lenny's voice breaks his train of thought.

"We all know what hair is, but I do not have a clue what any of these other objects contain, even though I have some ideas. Control, can you please analyse all these objects and make your analysis available to all as a separate report?"

A message appears on all the screens" 'Yes, Lenny, it will be completed within ten minutes'.

"Thank you, Zedon. Okay then, let us now read this ancient letter." With that, Zedon displays the letter across the media network.

Lenny takes a deep breath, holds it for a moment, then lets it out slowly. Tens of millions follow his example without even realising it.

Lenny feels it is his duty to lead the reading.

> "45 Melville Crescent
> Chelterton
> 15 August 2012
> My name is Pablo Adam."

About two billion people follow the letter on the screens in front of them.

Lenny continues reading, "It is now 19h35. I just arrived home from work a short while ago. As I pulled into my driveway, I felt something was wrong. My dog, Killer, was not outside to greet me. When I got to the front door, it was unlocked. When I opened the door, my entire family was lying on the ground, dead. My wife, sweet Melanie, was shot in the head. Our daughter, the bright and ever cheerful Madeleine—nineteen years old—dead, lying in a pool of her own blood. Our son, Brumin, twenty-one years old—dead, shot in the leg and in the head. Killer, bleeding from a wound in his side, was sitting by them, making the sorriest moaning sounds I have ever heard, licking their faces. I covered them with blankets. It was the hardest thing I ever had to do.

"I decided not to live on without them and I hope God will forgive me for what I am about to do. There is no longer any point to my life. I decided to honour my family by making up this time capsule in which we can be together. I also placed in it something from each one of us—something we each loved.

"Melanie, I am so sorry. I have not been the best husband I could be. Now I will never have the chance to make up for lost time. Madeleine, my angel, I am so sorry I wasn't here to protect you. Brumin, my son, I am sorry it had to end this way. May we meet again.

"To whoever opens this time capsule—please handle our memories and our sorrow with great care.

"Pablo Adam."

It was a gargantuan struggle for Lenny to complete the reading of the letter, as his voice broke after every few lines. His heart settled in his throat and it was only his sense of duty that caused him to complete the task. He walks backwards to his chair—like a sleepwalker—sits down and uses all his might to resist lowering his face into his hands, but he cannot control the shiver that runs up and down his spine.

There was not a dry eye in the hall or in front of any media screen. The stunned silence belies the trepidation welling up under the surface as the substance of the letter sinks in. Lenny, realising he has responsibilities, stands up in silence for an awkward moment, then his mouth opens, but nothing comes out.

He coughs. "Fellow assemblers, let us observe a minute of silence for this family, which was destroyed so brutally."

But most people do not respond—he cannot understand what is going on. The consternation gives way to an ominous silence and he follows the numerous eyes to the screen behind him. Comments are streaming thick and fast at the bottom of the screens,

'Oh no! How horrible!'
'How could people do this to each other?'
'Those poor people!'
'I cannot deal with this!'
'This is too much to bear!'
'I do not understand what is going on!'
'How senseless . . .'
'This is too painful!'

It is an endless stream of woe . . .

As he reads, Lenny feels jaws of steel slowly squeezing his chest. As he absent-mindedly rubs over his heart, Jodi whispers something in his ear, thereby waking him from his semi-stupor.

"Control informs me that over two hundred million viewers have responded already and the flow of interactions continues to be of an exceptionally high degree—two hundred and fifty million now. Ninety-six percent of respondents appear totally exasperated. It seems as if this information is causing an unprecedented and unhealthy outpouring of anguish."

'I feel sick.'
'How could we broadcast such information—have we gone mad?'
'Someone, make it stop!'

Gerry is mesmerised by the comments; his alarm grows exponentially as he continues to read.

'So many senseless deaths. I am aghast. How could people do this to each other? I cannot watch any further . . .'
'Oh no! That poor family! So much suffering! I am shocked!'

'This is totally debilitating!'

Gerry suddenly begins to feel agitated and scared as his thoughts flow to his partner, Annebelle—how did she receive these terrible tidings? Thank goodness the council prevented children from viewing the live broadcast. A lot of people normally respond to important broadcasts, but never before was such a huge reaction witnessed. He does not know what to make of the dangerous note of shock and despondency that is streaming in from across the globe. Yet they merely bring forth thoughts and feelings that threaten to whirl out of control in his own head and bosom.

His beeper goes off and he touches his wrist communicator—a shiny big metallic coin, held in place by a bejewelled bracelet. The surface of the coin opens to reveal a thin screen, across which a message from Council Control flashes. It is a request for the council to convene first thing in the morning to take stock of the effect of the opening of the capsule. He whispers his agreement and two minutes later Lenny informs the house of the council's meeting.

He continues, "Council Control is concerned about the state of affairs now existing and wishes to address the population. Over to you, Control."

Zedon moves to the front of the stage.

"Greetings to all. In the past twenty minutes, we received 1.2 billion responses. Eighty percent of respondents reveal utter despair of such a high intensity that immediate intervention is required on a large scale. In the absence of a council meeting, a message has just gone out to all councillors to vote whether Council Control should assume the responsibility to intervene in the situation until the council comes together tomorrow morning."

As he talks, the votes of individual councillors populate the media screens.

"It has just been confirmed to me that all the councillors agree with the proposal. Council Control is at this very moment mobilising an additional half a million humandroid psychologists to provide professional support to all those who may need it.

They will be available for duty within another thirty minutes. We strongly urge all who may feel the need to access their services. The first television channel will be cleared for their use exclusively. All PAs will be tuned in to their frequency. Therefore, to access them, all you have to do is ask your PA. PAs will also recommend counselling if they think you may need it. All PAs have also been put on temporary total mode—as this is the first time this is done, an explanation of what it entails will be streamed across all media screens throughout the evening. It is recommended that the assembly adjourns so that all delegates can go home to comfort and support their families and, in turn, receive the same. I wish you well for the night ahead."

"Thanks, Zedon. On this unfortunate note then, I hereby adjourn the assembly till further notice . . . go well."

The back and left walls slowly ascend into the roof, allowing the mass of heavy hearts to depart within minutes without causing any serious congestion. Gerry works his way through the throng to Lenny, who is still standing on the stage studying the gigantic media screen. "Good evening, old buddy, what a situation! How are you holding up?"

"Hi, Gerry. I really don't know. I just want to get home and lie down, my mind is a veritable fog! Have we let some demons out tonight! I have a terribly portentous feeling about all of this. What about you, are you okay?"

"I feel sick, to tell you the truth, and as worried as a fly in a beehive concerning Annabelle . . . . I have to get to her. Look after yourself, I will see you in the morning."

Gerry takes his leave. Once outside, he walks across the lawn that surrounds the hall, looking out for his travellor, which he knows will find him, with his pilot—the humandroid, Aaron—at the helm.

People board their travellors hectically, then swish and swoosh off urgently into the twilight.

Aaron promptly lowers the travellor in front of Gerry, who hops aboard as soon as the passenger door slides open.

"Hi Aaron! It's a prorogue, are we travelling alone?"

"Yes, Gerry, it appears that no one else is going in our direction, and hi to you too."

He puts himself down on the seat next to his pilot, who notices that he is quite downcast. He accesses the travellor's media unit, looking for the message promised by Council Control—here it is, in bold letters.

"The Annals of the Simplicity of Life of 3079 restricted the duties that PAs or any other humandroids may perform for their families. They may not handle food and drink, clean kitchens or ablution facilities, nor may they look after children for more than two hours in any one day. The reason for this is to avert a situation where the comforts of society give rise to a complacent and supercilious people incapable of looking after themselves. Should such a situation come to pass, it would be a crime against our own humanity. All these restrictions are now lifted until further notice."

"Ah, Aaron, I see I'm going to be spoilt rotten."

"It would be my pleasure to help, Gerry, and it is a good decision too."

Gerry cannot imagine an existence without Council Control. It is a huge, complex computer system with a mobile as well as an immobile component. The latter is a huge building complex stacked with interconnected computer brains that are linked to myriad lesser controls across the globe and beyond. The walls of the rooms contain its main power sources, as well as its reserve power units. The mobile components are Jodi, Zedon and Nicole, the last being the face of Council Control and its leading component. All three of them serve and maintain the immobile core and update it continuously. They are, in fact, independent super, super computers in their own right. Council Control answers only to the Council of the Realm. Yet, despite all of these resources, the council was still stumped by a rusty, tiny, dolorous box. As if with a jerk, his mind conjures up a picture of Gaston. Poor Gaston . . . He must reassure him . . .

"Hi, Gaston . . ."

CHAPTER 2

─━━•᠁⊶⊷◦⟨⊙⟩◦⊶⊷᠁•━━─

Dark Soul

Gerry listens to the quiet hum of the engine as he reclines in his seat, the recent proceedings very much on his mind. Annabelle! He quickly contacts his life partner. Within a blink, her pleasant image appears on the screen in front of him.

"Hi, Gerry." She waves meekly as she greets him. "Hi, Aaron."

He sits up—she didn't call him 'sweetheart' like always. He notices deep, unfamiliar lines in her otherwise delicate and serene face. She is not her usual cheerful self. He is worried.

"Hello, my lovely. I wish you were here with me, have you been missing me?" When she does not return his greeting immediately, he continues nervously, "The contents of the time capsule turned out to be a real bombshell, our world has been turned topsy-turvy. You do not look quite yourself, dearest . . . tell me how you feel." She still does not reply, but he sees a strange contortion of the muscles in her face. "As for me, I am still pretty gob-smacked, if you will pardon the euphemism."

Her face suddenly breaks up and a torrent of tears streams down her cheeks, yet she makes no sound. He never saw her cry before, but this is beyond crying! He feels absolutely desperate.

"Annie, darling, Annie, talk to me please." His voice is a plea. "Aaron, when is the soonest we can arrive?"

"In one hour, Gerry."

With that, the pilot increases their speed tenfold and Gerry feels his seat adjusting to parry the sudden forward thrust. Annabelle weeps helplessly . . .

He just looks at her, her mouth open. She is a deluge of tears, she shakes her head, turns around and leaves the room.

He must get to her! She is descending into an abyss . . . he must get to her.

"PA! PA!" he shouts frantically into the screen.

A friendly looking humandroid appears. Gerry tells him of his concerns for his partner and asks him to be very vigilant and to make sure that she is okay.

"What is she doing now, PA?"

"She is lying on your bed, crying; the personal medic is talking to her. I am busy connecting her with Psychological Support Services."

"Thanks, PA. I am less than an hour away. I rely on you, old friend."

PM, or personal medic, is the name for the medical component built into all beds. PM diagnoses people while they lie on the bed or sleep on it, able to apply a variety of light treatments that include aromatherapy, massages, selective heating therapy and magnetic rehabilitation—while they sleep—for myriad medical problems. Every morning, everybody's PM gives her or him a diagnostic medical report that includes treatments applied during the evening and recommendations for further treatment or care as may be required. Every PM interfaces uninterruptedly with PM Control, which maintains a medical database of every individual and that, in turn, is connected to Medical Care Control.

Gerry sends PA a text message: 'please keep me apprised of every change that may occur, no matter how small—thanks'.

"I need to calm down . . . there is a maelstrom inside me. I will be of no use to Annie if I am in a state myself." He realises he is thinking out loud. *Must get this anxiety under control; do not think of what may happen. Gather your strength for when you will really need it*—he 'talks' to himself in this trend until Aaron—who senses his stress—interrupts his thoughts.

Although Aaron is a pilot, like all humandroids he is very versatile and senses that his companion is in need of calming conversation. "What about a calming beverage, Gerry?"

"Oh, good idea . . . I'll get it myself." He gets up, goes to the kitchen and returns with a cup of honey tea.

"That time capsule is really quite something, eh, Gerry? People in the distant past really had to contend with major tragedies."

"Yes, Aaron. I wish I could also just cry like Annabelle—I certainly feel like it. My emotions are a convoluted mess. My head seems to take in these senseless killings—yet my heart, my entire being, is crying out against it—like it is trying to repel everything I heard and saw in the assembly . . . like it wants to put everything back into the box! I cannot explain my state of mind. And I am afraid, Aaron, afraid that we are merely witnessing the harbinger of an event or chain of events of cataclysmic proportions that will be confronting us on the morrow."

"I understand your concerns and share them. I searched all databases for evidence of crises of analogous proportions in the past thousand years, but found none. Society is confronted by a situation completely unchartered. I suggest, Gerry, that you talk to someone at Psychological Support Services; it can only help you and prepare you better to be of assistance to Annabelle. I can open the channel for you."

"Maybe I should. Thanks, it's a good idea . . . Do so, Aaron."

He was shocked at the incoherence and intensity of his own outpourings when the psychologist asked him to put all his feelings into words. The psychologist, Meremezi, listened patiently and made calculated interventions. After talking and talking, he felt totally spent and his mind went blank.

"The situation has exposed a veritable chasm," soothes Meremezi, "between the people of the twenty-first century and modern humans. In the former era, death and destruction were heaped on people by other people as part of daily life. Genocide, war, government-sponsored secret killings, mass murder, criminal deaths and suicides were the order of the day. This millennia-old orgy of blood and destruction was glorified in literature, was re-enacted in countless movies, television programmes and even children's games. Books for little children many times centered on giants or ogres killing children only to be killed in turn by someone else. This attitude of accommodation acculturated murder. In other words, people were forced to accept this as the normal state of affairs. Humanity has known nothing of this for thousands of years, hence, though modern humans can deal with this information from the point of view of distant history and education, the psyche of the modern person appears incapable of bridging this chasm once this brutal reality in the form of specific, living victims, has touched the modern heart."

Meremezi's voice has an almost hypnotic effect on Gerry, causing him to relax and close his eyes. He drifts off into a numbing sleep, but wakes up after just a few minutes.

"Thank you, Meremezi, I feel much more at ease now."

After terminating the session, he mulls over the words of the psychologist. He is amazed at the amount of research that has ostensibly been done in such a small period of time by the various control centres, though a number of his specific questions could not be answered yet as more time is needed for research, given that the Adam family lived so long ago. A lot of research will have to be done—and will be done—before clarity will be obtained about the society of Mister Adam and his family. He presses peremptorily on his personal communicator.

"PA, how is she doing?"

"She is still lying on the bed and crying softly, Gerry; I cannot get any response from her so I am just watching over her."

"Thanks, PA, see you soon."

He jumps off the travellor before it comes to a complete stop and half runs through the front door, past PA with a quick 'hi' and comes to a stop in the doorway of their bedroom. She is lying in the foetal position, sobbing softly. "Annie!" The soft cry rips through his chest. He kicks of his shoes, goes around the massive bed and sits next to her with his feet on the bed, lifts her up under her arms and pulls her against him. "Oh, my lovely Annie . . ." he mumbles softly and he does not even realise that his own tears are mixing with hers.

The upper end of the bed rises slowly to support his back. With her face against his chest and his face in her hair, she stops sobbing and, without saying a word, her hand slowly reaches up to his cheek, stroking it softly. So they fall asleep, Gerry and Annabelle, in a tender embrace, trying to keep the gathering tempest at bay. As sleep whisks him off, he decides that sleep is probably the best remedy for Annabelle right now; he will connect her with a psychologist in the morning before he leaves for the meeting.

On instruction from PM, the bed straightens out very slowly, so as not to disturb their sleep and, like a good nurse of old, PM ensures that they have a good night's rest. In his semi-delirious sleep, Gerry's mind jerks between images of his sleeping beloved, murderous mayhem and the looming council meeting.

CHAPTER 3

———— •⸗•◦◦◦•⸗• ————

Anguish from the Abyss

G erry listens to his medical report on the media screen in the kitchen while enjoying his early snack. He is eating alone this morning—Annabelle having said she will breakfast later. "You're in good health, Gerry, but I have a few concerns. Your frame of mind is not balanced or calm. I applied aromatherapy during the evening to enhance deep sleep, but your condition is tied up with the anomalous situation arising from the reading of Mister Adam's letter. I will continue with aromatherapy at night until the entire situation is resolved, but I would also like you to continue with treatment from Psychological Support Services. Furthermore, my tenth reminder, you need to reduce your alcohol intake by one third, because you are at risk of micro-level cell damage if you don't. Your current average of three glasses per week is detrimental to your health in the long run and should be reduced to two. Would you like further details?"

"No, no, PM, I remember what you said yesterday and yes, I will cut down on my beloved pulque, but I must add that you make me sound like a real dipsomaniac!"

"I do not mean to in the least . . ."

Gerry laughs. "Just pulling your leg, PM. Don't worry, from now on only dram for me! And, thanks for taking care of

Annabelle, she seems to have slept well. Oh, look at the time! Have to go to my meeting."

"Have a good journey and meeting, Gerry."

Before departing, he goes back to Annabelle. "Are you awake, love?"

She sits up and beckons to him to sit next to her. She puts one arm around his shoulder, puts her face against his chest and touches his cheek, her favourite position. *She still looks tired,* he thinks.

"Annie, PA will arrange a session for you with a psychologist, is that in order with you?"

She notes the concern in his tender, loving voice. She feels plain horrible for causing him such worry, but she just cannot help it. "Thanks, Gee. I will be all right; off to your meeting you go." She sits up straight and smiles wryly, but her attempt at bravado fools him not in the least.

With a kiss, he takes his leave.

Once in the travellor, piloted again by Aaron, he realises that he did not yet take the time to weigh up the events of the day before.

He cannot think of anything worse than the killing of one human being by another. Humans are such amazingly wonderful, powerful, dignified and beautiful beings. What can cause one person to fire a projectile into the body of another with the idea to rip and tear flesh and bone until life itself is extinguished? How does someone plunge a sharp object into the flesh of another— causing the victim's blood and very life to ooze out of his or her body?

Every part of the human body is delicate and so full of energy, life and feeling—to inflict harm on a human being is simply beyond his cognitive ability. As these thoughts twirl around in his brain, he has to fight back a sudden feeling of nausea and panic.

What about all those people who responded last night? Hopefully they are fine after a good night's rest? Or is this wishful thinking? Is the crisis behind us or does a minatory period lie ahead? Surprisingly, Council Control did not update him on the situation during the night—and he assumes this goes for all the other councillors—is that good or bad?

"Aaron, my good friend, you must have had a busy night."

The pilot chuckles, "And how, Gerry! I do not think so much research was ever done during a single evening. It was a night of terabytes and zilobytes—all computers were stretched to their limits! And, Gerry, I just lapped up everything that was sent to my databases. I think I now know everything there is to know about the time of the Adams."

"Amazing, Aaron." He manages a laugh with difficulty. "What is the main feeling you get from their era?"

"The main feeling is one of surprise at the manifold contradictions. For instance, society then was extremely advanced scientifically, yet humanity was very backward philosophically, socially, psychologically and morally. In my opinion, people back then lived not according to principles based on humanity, but on ones based on something I can only call inhumanity. I know this sounds harsh, Gerry . . ."

"Harsh, certainly, but you pricked my curiosity . . . Expound your statement a little."

"Humans were so advanced that they regularly sent spaceships and probes on missions. They commanded the wealth and capacity to provide for all the basic needs (and more) of the entire population of the world. But what did they do? A tiny elite managed to control the wealth of the Earth and had all their needs and desires catered for, whereas the overwhelming majority of people lived on inadequate portions of what was needed to merely keep life and limb together. Can you believe, Gerry, that people were dying on a daily basis from hunger while this elite were leading lives of grandeur?"

"This is very strange, shocking indeed, impossible for me to understand, for no one today will be able to eat if there is one human being who does not have food . . . Oh, Aaron, what have we done? The Adams era scares me. Of course I understand your argument now, Aaron. I think I will close my eyes for a while. Wake me up fifteen minutes before arrival, Aaron, please."

"Will do, Gerry."

He lowers his seat into bed format and its soothing vibrations cause him to fall asleep within minutes. But it feels to him as if he is falling down a deep gorge.

He walks into the summit room with five minutes to spare. Each councillor is sitting at a conference desk. These are special desks, situated around a humungous, fat, circular metallic dome covered with wood with a deep mahogany tinge. Each desk is fitted with its own chair, a media screen mounted on the left, a keyboard built into the front section with two glasses behind it—each under the thin spout of a faucet that issues from the dome—to the right of the keyboard is a place for books and next to that a few electronic gadgets, including a set of tiny, wireless earphones. To Gerry, the unprecedented amount of vacant seats is a worrying portent. The face of Council Control, Nicole, is in attendance. Her normally pleasant, smiling face has been displaced by a stern countenance as if to prepare the councillors for what is to come.

She opens the meeting with greetings. This responsibility is normally the function of a councillor, but, given that Council Control has been managing the crisis since the night before, it is incumbent on it to initiate the proceedings.

"First of all, Councillors, Control recommends that the proceedings of the meeting not be broadcast openly, as information to be revealed here may lead to more despair amongst the population. What we suggest is that those who would like to follow the proceedings put in a request and Control will broadcast the proceedings to their personal communicators after ensuring that they can cope with the information."

Though this would be the first time proceedings of a council meeting would not be broadcast openly with opportunities for the population to interact with the meeting, the proposal was quickly accepted. She continues with urgency,

"In the aftermath of last night's assembly, a further two hundred million people responded to Council Control. The responses were generally the same—shock, trepidation, dismay and despair—at the contents of Mister Adam's letter. The responses can be grouped into varying degrees of the above. During the night, personal medics from around the world reported very disturbing trends.

"Over half the population could not sleep the night before, despite treatment by their PMs. The morning found sixty percent of the citizenry with varied combinations of symptoms such as deep sorrow, extreme emotional sensitivity, fatigue, body aches, moodiness, nausea and/or vomiting, slurred speech, impaired coherence, heart palpitations, a weakened immune system and a serious sense of hopelessness. Medical Care Control has so far determined that all these conditions together are but symptoms of a single disorder; what it is they cannot say yet, but are working on it as we speak. The link between these symptoms and the assembly is clear, but the personal medics are not equipped to properly diagnose—let alone treat—such an unknown condition. Due to the numbers so afflicted, this is clearly a pandemic. The Controls of the various labour departments reported this morning that the vast majority of their human workforces are absent from work today, with only a fraction of them having called in sick. Twenty-five percent of the members of this very council are so affected and three quarters of them apologised for their absences today. The entire society is in turmoil. The situation is fluid and we do not know how it will unfold further. And now I will pause for a moment, as I would like you to brace yourselves for the rest of my report."

Gerry wonders how he must brace himself if he feels like a sack of jelly. What can be worse? There is more to come? He is not sure if he really wants to hear anymore.

Nicole continues, "One hour ago, two people in South America who displayed severe variations of the symptoms ended their own lives . . ."

Pandemonium prevents her from continuing. Councillors at wits end jump up, sit down, jump up again look at each other for help and break into a Babylonian babble, some tugging at their hair.

"Friends! Friends!" Gerry's quavering, yet peremptory, cry brings the tumult to a halt, and he continues with a voice as heavy as his soul, "Has ever there been a situation so dire to face? Has ever there been a situation that so earnestly called on us for wisdom, calm and resolve? Believe me, this is only the beginning of our suffering. Let this poignant tale of woe not be our undoing. It is now the time to strengthen our hearts and confront the demons of our adversity. I say, let Nicole complete her report, what say you?"

Gerry wipes the tears from his face and is himself taken aback by the eloquence and power of his oratory. After murmurs of acquiescence, Lenny thanks Gerry for re-focussing the councillors on the task at hand and beseeches them further to be prepared for worse to come. Gerry gazes thankfully upon his friend's face as Lenny takes his seat with shoulders hunched and head drooping. *Gosh, how old he looks now. What will become of us . . .*

After answering a barrage of questions, Nicole continues by outlining the measures put forward by Council Control for the meeting's consideration. Gerry's mind keeps wandering. Good grief! People are starting to kill themselves now? Gerry thinks about Annabelle . . . PA will inform him if there is any change in her behaviour, but he must get back quickly. PA has been texting him messages every thirty minutes since he left the house. Killing themselves . . . ? The report added greatly to Gerry's disquiet and to that of all the members present. The rest of the meeting was a haze as Gerry tried to shake off feelings of despair closing in on him.

When he finally arrives home, Gerry goes to check on his life partner without delay. He finds her sleeping and brushes her forehead ever so gently with his lips—at pains not to wake her. He is tired from the long journey and from the confusion in his head. Yet he pushes resting from his mind. He asks PA to put a camera in the room and relay the image to his wrist. Then he goes into the garden, where the greenery, trees, array of colourful flowers, iridescent ladybirds and butterflies help him to calm his thoughts. The scene is simply surreal in the soft, golden glow of the late afternoon sun. The garden is the size of the plot the house is on, large enough for short walks through the trees, flowers, ponds and bird baths. On the outskirt, close to the back door of the house, two long and comfortable benches can be found, with footrests for six people.

Instead of sitting on the bench where he can normally be found when in the garden, he simply walks up and down, looking at his wrist every few minutes. He shakes his head vigorously to clear it.

"PA," he calls into his personal communicator. "Please come to the garden."

"Can I be of any assistance, Gerry?"

"Of course, my friend, how did Annie's consultation with the psychologist go, and did she eat at all while I was gone?"

"She never got out of bed. I took her some food on five occasions—the first time, she did not even touch it, the second time, she just tasted a morsel, then she did not eat again. I suggest you request a nurse to take care of her. She terminated her session with the psychologist after one minute only."

"Good idea about the nurse, PA. Arrange it for me please. Try to put her in touch with a psychologist again tomorrow, please. On another note, are you aware of the proceedings of today's council meeting?"

"No, Gerry."

"I need you to help me think things through—you know I admire your exactitude. I will ask Council Control to update you."

He proceeds to speak into the disc on his wrist.

One minute later. "I am fully updated, Gerry."

"The briefing was really too much for me to deal with in my present state. The council adopted the recommendations of Control, but I'm not sure I absorbed the full sweep thereof. Refresh my memory for me."

"Council Control made preparations for the setting up of a global humandroid committee with a special Control centre called Pandemic Control, which will be dedicated to the twin objective of uncovering the medical cause or causes of the pandemic and developing the best possible treatment. The brief of the committee will be as fluid as the situation. While the committee does its work, council meetings will continue by means of video conferencing. The next council meeting will be set up once Pandemic Control is ready to report back. Continuous update reports on the global situation will be made available to all council members, and Council Control will dispatch nannies to assist families with pre-teens.

"Personal medics will also use their discretion to induce sleep in people whom they regard as a danger to themselves, for twenty-four hours at a time until further notice and, in such cases, nurses will administer intravenous feeding. Gerry, the recommendations were endorsed in full."

"Thanks, buddy, and I expect the committee's work will be supererogatory; I got my first update report on my journey back home—four persons in Japan and two persons in Europe had, by then, killed themselves, PA. Twenty minutes ago, I got another update of a man in Mother Africa who ended his own life!"

Despite trying very hard, he cannot hide the fear in his voice. They talk for a while, Gerry rambling on and PA listening patiently.

"The nurse is here, Gerry, I will let her in and brief her."

"Thanks. I will wait here for you."

Gerry winces as the update report tone beeps on his wrist. One person committed suicide in North America and one in Asia Minor.

PA returns. "Gerry, I am also getting the updates. People taking their lives with their own hands like this is something as new to me as it is to everybody else on the planet. Yet, information from the databases indicates that this practice is as old as humanity itself. Throughout history, people sacrificed themselves for various reasons—to protect their children and other loved ones, for a noble cause, to escape pain and suffering, and also arising from a multitude of psychological causes. The last suicide occurred four thousand and eleven years ago. The best thing to do now is to wait for Pandemic Control to report. If the updates disturb you, Gerry, I suggest you ask Council Control to bypass you. Should I bring you a calming beverage?"

"I cannot ask for a bypass, PA. I have to do my duty, no matter how tough. My goodness, PA, I do not know what to think anymore—if only I could say a requiescat! This is all so wrong . . . and what about Annabelle? Yes please, I'll take some warm coconut cocktail . . . I really need it, thanks."

He drinks his beverage in the garden, walking up and down, while PA watches him with concern. "What do we do now, PA? Not only must we find a way of firstly stopping these suicides, we must heal everybody and protect society from further harm. How will we be able to process all these deaths if we cannot even deal with the deaths of the Adam family? How many more people will die before the situation stabilises? Can our world be redintegrated?"

PA does not reply, as he realises his friend is merely thinking out loud. He hears the hollowness in his companion's voice; is he going to fall ill too? He knows he has to be extremely patient and help him to focus his mind on the task at hand and he hopes the storm proves to be but a squall.

At last, Gerry sits down, adjusts the bench, puts his feet on an ottoman, leans back and slowly snoozes off.

PA sits on the small bench next to Gerry's that completes an L-shape, and looks ponderingly at his patron, how vulnerable he looks . . . PA, named Silvio, has been with Gerry and Annabelle since the two got married. A PA—short for personal assistant—is a feature of every household. A humandroid robotic creation that services the household in various ways. Its most important task is to keep the family connected with Council Control and all other relevant databases. They are receptionists of their homes and also act as companions to their families. They are supercomputers and amazingly versatile—they can sing like birds, paint like Picasso, debate like Socrates and run like the wind. As mentioned before, their duties are proscribed by law, in as far as they are not allowed to serve people with food or drink, clean kitchens or ablution facilities, nor may they look after children for more than two hours in any one day. A life without their PAs is unimaginable to modern humankind.

Gerry stirs lightly. PA looks at him with soft eyes as he changes his position on the bench, dressed in a beige shokta—a loose and flowing one-piece suit that is actually a single, intelligent sheet that forms itself into an outfit as soon as the head is pushed through it. His shoes, constructed mainly from energy—as all modern shoes are—are kicked out and look like two soles in their switched-off mode. He looks great for his fifty-five years with his tall and slender frame and powerful build, with that characteristic spring in his step that all good athletes have, being an excellent international soccer player and marathon runner in his age group. He is a philosopher fourth grade, and currently doing research on mysticism and its social functions through the ages. The research is in its second year and still far from completion. Gerry is a bit of a shy fellow and very passionate about everything he is involved in. Highly capable in whatever he tackles, he is an excellent organiser and a natural leader. He never speaks ill of anyone and is charm, grace and sophistication itself. His compassion knows no bounds and, like a typical modern human being, he is driven by the desire to expand his knowledge and that of society. Despite his serious personality, Gerry is gregarious, quite affable and can be very funny in company, especially around children.

CHAPTER 4

•═╍═◦◖◗◦═╍═•

Gaston's Rue

G aston is one of the last to leave the assembly and he does so in a cloud of sombreness. His thoughts are self-torturing. *Is this all my fault? Should I have thrown the capsule away?* Such thoughts whirl and twirl through his head as he hops into his travellor, piloting being one of his joys.

As he whizzes off, the travellor's media screen blinks and Gerry looks at him, hailing him.

"Hello, Gerry."

"Gaston, I flashed in just to make sure you are all right. Having found the box, I can imagine how easily you can blame yourself for this calamity. I hope you are not. Well, are you . . . ?"

"Look, Gerry, I honestly feel just terrible about the situation. I know I cannot blame myself because I am just like the proverbial messenger with the bad news, but I just cannot shake off this feeling of guilt. I think I'll be okay in a day or two."

"If we want to blame anyone, we should blame the council, who was clearly unwise to open the capsule in public. But how could we know that a little rusty box and the past could be so toxic? Nay, Gaston, no one is at fault here. The box was just a catalyst, it unlocked and set into motion something that has been lurking in the bosom of humanity since times primitive, but that modern humanity never dealt with properly. This is the nub of the matter and this is what we need to deal with. I suggest that you talk to someone at Psychological Services, my young friend."

"All right, Gerry, I will do so. Thanks for your encouragement. It helps a lot. I will survive, don't worry . . . ."

"Okay then, safe journey."

"Bye."

Gaston wonders why people say 'safe journey'; no journey has been unsafe for as long as he can remember. He presses a key on the communications portal. "Hi, Junaid, do some research for me please . . . why do we say 'safe journey' to people who travel? Where does this come from?"

Junaid is his PA and is only too happy to be of service. "Will do, Gaston. Must I make my presentation when you arrive or while you are still in transit?"

"When I arrive, my friend, see you then."

His mind jumps incoherently from one thought to the next until it settles on the day the capsule was discovered.

He was part of a construction team that excavated a large area for the construction of new houses. The team before them demolished the buildings and removed the rubble. It was a wintry sort of day in the heart of autumn. There was not a patch of blue in the sky. And strangely, all sorts of birds flew over the site in large flocks throughout the day, making strange beckoning sounds. He remembers that the extraordinary context grabbed his attention. As he scooped up another heap of earth with the grotesque limb of the giant excavator, he saw the rusty box on its media screen; every scoop is x-rayed and projected on the screen and the pilot has to use his or her discretion when something of interest is revealed. The box certainly pricked his curiosity and he retrieved it quickly. He called the rest of his team and they discussed what they thought it could be.

"Well . . ." said Darius, stating the obvious, "it is certainly very old."

Gaston grabbed a tool and there and then wanted to break the box open, but bethought himself and realised that it could possibly contain an ancient relic or two. He contacted Council Control, and, within an hour, a travellor came to fetch it.

They all watched the travellor depart with its rusty cargo, when suddenly flashes of lightning, then thunder accompanied its ascent. That signalled the end of the day's work.

Why are all those natural coincidences suddenly in his mind? In bygone epochs, they would certainly have been regarded as omens. He shivers. He has to shake off these feelings and thoughts—*we must hope against hope*. He tunes in to Psychological Services.

CHAPTER 5

❧❦❧

Report

G erry gets a start when his wrist beeps. *Come on, Gerry, focus! You need to be strong now.* "Twenty-five members of the council reported sick within the past hour."

Gerry continues to walk up and down; he does not notice the hours passing by or the chill rustling in on the back of the breeze. As time goes by, his thoughts become more and more desultory. The emergency beep jerks him back to reality. Pandemic Control is ready to report. All available council members are to open the media conferencing portals in their media rooms.

As soon as he enters the media room, Gerry can barely contain his excitement as he blurts, "Video conferencing on!"

A screen emanates from the media crystal attached to the wall in front of them and forms an almost colourless ball—the hologram sphere—that reaches from the floor right up to the ceiling.

PA watches as Gerry pitapats detachedly on the side of the settee as they wait for the conference to begin. At last . . .

Nicole runs the proceedings. "Councillors, unfortunately the bad news is not over. Since this morning, reports of suicides were received from around the world. Latest reports put the total figures at ten citizens in Africa, fifteen citizens in the Americas, eighteen citizens in Asia, five citizens in Australasia and seven citizens in Antarctica. Yes, Gerry?"

"Did you find out the cause of this pandemic yet?"

"Pandemic Control is ready to report, Gerry. Council Control is satisfied that they have come up with an accurate description of the nature and causes of the pandemic, and fully supports their recommendations. Before that happens, Council Control wants us to discuss the weak attendance at this conference. Only fifty-five of the hundred council members are present—the others are all sick."

"We note the absences, can we decide after we hear the report?" Gerry asks again.

"Agreed! Ninety percent is in favour. I hand over to Stanislow, the representative of Pandemic Control."

A swarthy humandroid who has the appearance of a serious, but handsome, middle-aged man, with thick hair underlined by a cochineal cravat, takes his place at the podium.

"Dear Councillors, I greet you in these most trying of times. The Global Pandemic Committee completed research that took them back to the earliest relevant human records, which is an indication of the immense purview of their work. I present for your consideration their excellent report and I thank them again, on behalf of Pandemic Control, for their meritorious and speedy work. To view the report again later, you will need to request Pandemic Control Report one."

He notices that everyone nods to confirm.

"Very well then, this will take thirty minutes."

Gerry gets comfortable on his settee. PA brings him a demulcent drink on a tray and sits in the chair next to him.

Images appear in the sphere, with the presenter—life-sized—in the centre.

"Hello, Councillors, my name is Gracie, your host. If you have questions for me at any time during the presentation, just call my name . . . it is shown at the bottom of the sphere to your right."

With that, she vanishes, only to be replaced by Nicole.

She presents the prolegomenon of Council Control, which contextualises and endorses the report. For thirty minutes thereafter, the councillors are taken through the long-forgotten history of an illness unknown to humankind for thousands of years, the journey of the Global Pandemic Committee and its suggested solutions. Gerry intervenes frequently, asks numerous questions and plays Devil's Advocate until he is finally satisfied. The deliberations are extremely lengthy because all the councillors have numerous questions and many times Gracie has to arrange additional presentations on specific topics. After five hours of deliberations, the diminished conference agrees with all the recommendations. When Nicole adjourns the conference, Gerry switches the screen off, closes his eyes and slowly mulls over the most pellucid presentation he has ever experienced.

Depression, a disease that died out by itself several millennia ago. An illness that leads to people losing themselves, losing the wholeness of who they are. It can even lead to people taking their own lives without them knowing what they are doing. Now the entire society is paralysed by this peri-primitive disease. Medical treatment could control, but rarely cure it, especially not serious cases. The success rate of the treatment of serious cases in the twenty-first century was a meagre twenty-six percent. Most cases were, in fact, undiagnosed and, therefore, untreated. Some councillors expressed dismay at the lack of seriousness with which this disease was tackled in the past—many felt that the disease did not even have a proper medical name—again and again, the uncaring nature of peri-primitive society was bemoaned. We will not make the same mistakes. Now we will build on the achievements of the past and develop the treatments in line with our technology, philosophy and approach.

In peri-primitive times, medication was applied to restore chemical imbalances in the brains of the sick; this was a remarkable achievement. These medications will be modernised—including the nullification of all side effects—and they will be produced as inhalants and health beverages. Personal medics are being upgraded and, within one day, will be able to monitor and recommend treatment for brain chemical imbalances. The medication is already being finalised and will soon be mass produced.

The option of sleep inducement for citizens in danger is retained.

In the past, psychological counselling was a very crucial component of treatment; however, counselling had little effect in serious cases as both counsellor and patient had little power to remove most of the material causes of the depression, for instance, the uncaring nature of society, a serious lack of money, stressful jobs, past abuse or trauma, heartache, insensitive and uncaring parents or partners—these were examples mentioned in the presentation. The impotence of psychological counselling has been proven to be its acceptance of the broader status quo as the only possible reality; hence, it merely functioned to patch psychological scars with temporary band aids. In this way, it unintentionally helped to keep the wheels of the uncaring society going around and around.

Furthermore—and this suggestion momentarily ignited the house into a state of bedlam—the slain family will be regenerated, in other words, cloned. It is calculated by Pandemic Control that giving this family another chance at life will have immense therapeutic value that will also counteract the underlying causes of the imbalanced reproduction of neuro-chemicals. Society will be able to heal itself through caring for them and loving them.

Finally, a monument will be erected in honour of all humans who lost their lives as a result of the conscious acts of other humans. All people will be encouraged to visit the monument as soon as possible and annually thereafter. All senior educational institutions and all broadcast stations will develop philosophical programmes on the nature of the human being. It is hoped that this comprehensive intervention will wash away all the hurt and sorrow of the ages and allow modern people to reflect on humanity in the process of its historical unfolding. How did the narrator put it—*the past hangs like a dead horse around the shoulders of the present society.*

"This monument," she said, "will be society's honouring of all those victims who are screaming out to us through this calamity to remember them and their pain."

Another decision of the conference was inevitable. The Law of Relief was invoked. Forthwith, all humans are withdrawn from formal duty to society until further notice; their places will be taken over by humandroids. The Council of the Realm will continue functioning unless none of its members can function any longer, once the council's number drops below thirty percent, its functions will be taken over by Council Control. While Council Control holds this authority, it will be duty-bound to obtain the consent of all active councillors.

The report has reinvigorated him, he feels his perspicacity returning. Gerry still cannot decide if the council is partly responsible for what has happened. Opening the box in public . . . *Are we not too naïve at times? Has our society not become too smug in its comforts?* And what about the councils before? According to the report, the letter in the capsule was merely the last straw that unleashed this torrential outpouring. From a young age, we all learn about the senseless viciousness of person upon person in the distant past. Wars. Slavery. Criminal murders, Rape and assaults. Extra-judicial assassinations. Terrorism. It is estimated that people who lost their lives in this manner are five times the number of the current world population of 3.6 billion. But the heartrending demise of Mister Adam's family brought the reality of it all home with a vividness that could not be conjured by the wildest imagination.

There is lots of food for thought now. This crisis is forcing us to take a hard look at ourselves and to change some of our ways.

He feels the excitement building up in him. His heart races as he imagines seeing this family in front of him and interacting with them.

It is really an ingenious idea, and why not? Micro-cell memory technology can provide a regenerated human being with eighty percent of his or her memory labyrinth, and background context memory can be created through synthesised and distilled audio-image neuro-loading. A regenerated person will 'retain' ninety-five percent of his or her memory and character!

CHAPTER 6

— • ⚜ ◦❖◦ ⚜ • —

Against the Clock

T he world has become a barren, desolate landscape. Travellors that normally swoop everywhere are rarely seen nowadays. Citizens hardly leave their houses, many not even bothering to get out of bed. A gloomy mist has engulfed the length and breadth of the earth, bringing in its wake death and fear—fear of the unknown, fear for what tomorrow might bring. Fortunately, the suicides decreased greatly thanks to the interventions of Council Control.

But, amid all the despair, apathy, fear and funerals, the army of humandroids is busier than ever before, catering to their patrons' needs, fulfilling society's production requirements and keeping the blood of the civilisation flowing, its very heart pumping.

While all this is going on, there is a special team of men, women and humandroids at work in the main human sciences laboratory. Adam Family Scientific Team is a huge and well-resourced organisation. Led by Parween and Lyle, both in their forties and both philosophers fourth grade, the team has different departments. The cultural/social department is tasked firstly—but not only—with ensuring that the Adams are surrounded with culturally and socially familiar sights—objects and paraphernalia—when they ultimately emerge, at least for the first two weeks to facilitate their settling in. The regeneration department consists of four doctor-scientists, led by Egbert, and their assistants. To them falls the full responsibility of the actual cloning process, each one being responsible for one family member. The neuro-loading department is responsible for inputting the agreed memories and knowledge into the brains of each clone. They will work hand in hand with the cultural/social department, which will provide them with the necessary data. Finally, there is the settling-in department, which will decide on and arrange for where and how the Adams are to be accommodated. Each department has a number of humandroids who perform research, analytical, clerical and recording tasks, as well as whatever might be required of them.

The Adam Family Scientific Team has been granted lavish working space in the laboratory and most of its personnel can regularly be found working late into the evening, as the urgency of their tasks has not been lost on anyone.

Naturally, the team has its own control unit, namely, Adam Family Scientific Control Centre, which is directly connected to Council Control and all relevant databases.

Today is like any other day at the laboratory, with the exception that Lenny has decided to visit to get an on-the-ground feel for the progress made.

Lyle already took him to meet control and the personnel and to look at all the rooms the team is using. That is, all except the incubation rooms, as viewing a person being cloned is a taboo because it is regarded as a violation of such a person's privacy and integrity. The tour completed, Lyle takes him to the personnel rest room, where they find a number of staff members. After greetings all around, Lenny helps himself to some snacks and cool drink. "So Lyle . . ." begins Lenny, after finishing his bite. "Thanks from the bottom of my heart for the tour and update. Your team is doing a tremendous job and I can see that you are all equal to your responsibilities. I will take my leave now and will see you on the big day, which will be, as you said, in two weeks."

CHAPTER 7

• ·::·◦○❍○◦·::· •

Revivification

wo weeks later.

Eight council members are sitting in the especially renovated huge waiting room of the foremost human sciences laboratory, watching the unfolding situation on a huge media screen. All thirty-eight of the duty-fit members wanted to be present, but it was wisely thought their number would be intimidating.

They are watching four rooms simultaneously. Each Adam has his or her own room, which is sparsely furnished with a few chairs around a huge casket that rests on a low bed-like structure. The casket looks like a sarcophagus from a science fiction movie with its array of switches and blinking tiny lights rippling around its breadth in circles of different colours. Each family member is being tended to by a retinue consisting of one human doctor-scientist and two humandroids. At the fixed time, each doctor-scientist pushes a switch, then leaves the room. The caskets seem to lose their energy, the lights blinking for the last time and their covers simply disappearing—causing billions of necks to stretch in front of their media screens as they try to descry the caskets' contents. The occupants are gently injected with a substance that will wake them in exactly fifteen minutes, with a sense of tranquillity. For the first time ever, all media screens go grey as each person is picked up, carried to an adjacent room and put on a bed. The rooms are very typical for the epoch from which these newborns hail. Humandroids dress each in attire especially created for the occasion—albeit with modern materials—whereafter the doctor-scientists return and the media screens live again, this time broadcasting from the new rooms. In each room, the humandroids sit away from the bed and the doctor-scientist sits by the bed, holding the semi-conscious person's right hand . . . waiting patiently for him or her to rouse.

In the waiting room, not even breathing can be heard. The scene is replicated in houses across the world.

The awe and suspense is as thick as pea soup and can be felt from coast to coast, from continent to continent, from north to south, from east to west.

Brumin feels a slight prick. He suddenly feels he is waking up. Waking . . . Waking . . . from a dark and empty space. Images whirl around in his head. *They have a gun and knives . . . Leave my sister alone! No! Mommy! My leg!* Nothingness . . . He is gone again. The emptiness cascades back in concentric orbits. Where is he; in hospital? Where has he been—in a coma? So he survived? And Madeleine, and his mom

He has an urge to wake up . . . then a cloud whisks him away and a sense of calm oozes from his mind and spreads all over him, sinks into his clothes, into every pore of his skin . . . . His brain slowly starts to focus and completes the assimilation of the flurry of information that was loaded into his brain over the past five weeks. Good Lord—is all this for real? His eyes open, blink, blink, then close, then open again, stare. *Hello, Doctor.* His mouth opens, but nothing comes out. His throat is so dry . . . Try again. "Hello, Doctor . . . Are my mom and sister okay?" His voice is soft and sounds detached; he clears his throat and absent-mindedly rubs his right leg just above his knee. He looks at the bed, the other people in the room, his familiar clothes, then slowly sits up.

It was deemed advisable for the doctor-scientists to don the peri-primitive long white coat to reassure the members of the family.

"Hello, Brumin. Your family is doing just fine. I am a doctor and you are in good hands. My name is Egbert. Tell me how you feel."

"Very well, Doctor. Confused, but rested; my head feels heavy, though." "Your head will clear soon. You will meet your parents and sister shortly; we need to first do a few simple tests; is that all right with you?"

"Yes, sure, Doc, but I am famished."

The doctor laughs hesitantly. "Snacks will be provided in a short while and a little later you will attend a special banquet that has been prepared in honour of your family. We first need to dispense with a few preliminaries. Do you have any questions for me?"

"Maybe later, Doc; right now, my mind is too mixed up. I just want to see my family."

After some basic tests, each team brings its ward to an anteroom. In the waiting room and around the world, tears of joy trickle down billions of cheeks as this astonishing reunion is watched.

"Brumin, my son! Pablo! Maddie!"

"Mom, Mom, oh Mom!"

"Dad!"

"Maddie, Brumin, son!"

"Come here, brother!"

There are kisses, hugs and tears and more kisses, hugs and tears. The humandroids take their leave while only the doctor-scientists remain, waiting patiently with tears filling their eyes. The Adams hug and kiss each other in silence for what seems a very long time. Suddenly, they all stop and look at the doctor-scientists expectantly.

"Good afternoon, everybody, and welcome back . . ." Egbert was very proud when he was given this particular responsibility. He points to another room. "This room has been set aside for you to . . . perhaps . . . catch up? Please help yourself to the snacks. We will remain in this anteroom until you are ready; would you call us when you are?"

They go into the Adam Family Room without a further word.

From this moment, live broadcasts of images and sounds of the Adam family are no longer made, as, from here on, their permission is required.

Around the world, people take walks outside for the first time in months. They clear their heads as if waking from a terrible slumber. They greet each other felicitously—stop here to chat, stop there to prate. They breathe in the fresh air, the grass and flowers and hug the friendly trees. They take a new pleasure in the house art. They wave at the birds and butterflies and acknowledge the sky-hoppers who shout greetings to all and sundry. Then, with a spring in their steps, they hasten back, not to their media rooms this time, but to their kitchens or dining rooms—are they hungry! The PAs fall over their feet with joy as they bustle about trying to be of service. The food provision services are working at full steam like never before, with humandroids scurrying hither and thither to cope with the deliveries.

Gerry gets a start as his beeper goes off.

"Annabelle, sweetheart, how are you?"

"I feel great, Gerry, when can I expect you home? I miss you."

"I'm not sure, Annie. I miss you too. You certainly sound your affable self. What is that you are eating?" He always finds watching her eat very fascinating. She would break or scoop tiny morsels, put them into her mouth gracefully and chew like a little birdie.

"Pirozhki that dear PA organised for me . . . listen to this, he said he is going to spoil me today—I wonder what he thinks he has been doing every other day." She laughs; another characteristic of her that mesmerises him every time.

"I am so glad I have my own Annie back!"

"I will wait for you, so call me one hour before you arrive, okay?"

"Right, honey, bye now . . ." What a relief—his Annie is fine—she is fine, fine, fine. He is bursting with glee.

The Adams do not even see the snacks. They sit down quickly, holding hands.

"Listen . . ." starts Pablo. "They say we are not the same people, but are ninety-five percent the same in character and have ninety-five percent of our memories. I feel one hundred percent me! And you?"

Everybody—except Brumin—concurs.

"And you, Brumin?"

"Oh, me too . . . ."

His mother catches his eye momentarily, and mistakes his moroseness for grogginess.

"How did those bastards get in?" Pablo asks; he cannot hide the vexation in his voice.

The family talks about that dreadful night. It is clearly difficult and understandably traumatic for every one of them. No one notices the stiffening of Brumin's jaw while the topic is under discussion or how he rubs above his knee. In the end, they agree to leave that history behind them and focus on building their new lives.

"I am just so overjoyed to have all of you back again!" exclaims Melanie, and she hugs everyone.

Suddenly, their hunger decides to be ignored no longer and they start to tuck into the delectable, but tiny, snacks. They cannot get enough of the eats and drinks and keep on expressing their surprise to each other at the incredible and glorious tastes, or at the soft textures and colours. The snacks were finished all too quickly.

Egbert receives the Adams when they exit the room.

"We are at your service," says Pablo Adam to him. "Forgive me if I am a little flustered. We are not sure where to start . . . maybe you can tell us what is next?"

Egbert then introduces himself and the other three doctor-scientists properly. Each one will be responsible for one family member's medical requirements.

"We will all be going to the luncheon now. Present will be yourselves, eight members of the Council of the Realm and the four of us. You choose either we eat now or you first meet your personal assistants.

"Personal assistants first, please! We did have some snacks," pleads Madeleine.

Everyone laughs.

"Will they be showing us around?"

The doctor-scientists smile.

"Maddie, people are waiting for us . . ."

"What are another few minutes after so many years?" interjected Egbert. "It is no problem, Melanie; so be it then."

Four PAs come into the anteroom.

"Madeleine, this is your PA, Sipho. Pablo, this is your PA, Estienne. Melanie, this is your PA, Vida. Brumin, your PA is Boris."

"Hi all," greet the PAs in unison with a wave.

He then explains what a PA is and what its role is—the family is in total awe.

"But they look so, so totally human . . ." Melanie blurts out.

"How do we tell the difference between humandroids and humans?" chimed in Brumin.

Egbert laughs. "It is impossible without asking."

Scratching their heads, they go back into the Adam Family Room with their PAs to make each other's acquaintance.

"Look at you all! you look so perfect, my oh my . . . I cannot get over this!" She clutches the sides of her face as if to emphasise her surprise.

"Thank you, Melanie," says Vida.

Through his or her PA, the present society opens up to each Adam like a magical onion. They voraciously peel away layer after layer after layer. As the calming medication wears off, they feel their hearts beat excitedly in their throats ever so often. Then they are apt to catch a deep breath, bring themselves under control, and lap it up more and more. Pablo catches himself thinking—*so dying worked out very well for us, after all*—but he quickly shakes off so gross a thought. They start emerging after a full two hours—tired and hungrier than ever—not because their questions dried up, but out of consideration for those waiting for them.

When the doctor-scientists enter the specially prepared banquet room with their charges, they are met by the eight council members—all dressed like the Adams in denim jeans and an assortment of matching tee-shirts—at the entrance who shake their hands. No new introductions are made and they take their seats around a table that can seat twice as many as are in the room. The family sits together, two doctor-scientists on either side of them, then follow the council members. The atmosphere is quite amiable, with the councillors beaming from ear to ear. Brumin takes in the array of foods.

The middle section of the table rotates noiselessly and slowly, conveying an assortment of beverages, nuts, raisins and sliced fruit. There is a long counter against one wall, on which a variety of tantalising dishes beckon; against another wall, a smaller counter is adorned with various colourful salads in translucent porcelain bowls with ruby edges. Lenny taps a spoon against a glass to get everyone's attention.

"To Melanie, Madeleine, Brumin and Pablo, my name is Lenny and I welcome you to this banquet, but also to our society and your new lives. You met the doctor-scientists already. The other people present are Gerry, Fatima, Adele, Sulaiman, Vaxy, Yevgeny and Manuelle. Except for the doctor-scientists, we are all members of the Council of the Realm, a sort of committee that sits at the top of the administration of the world. This is your first proper meal in thousands of years and I wish you all *bon appetit!* Come, let us dish."

"Can I ask something?"

All eyes turn to Madeleine

"Of course, Madeleine, go ahead."

"I forgot to ask my PA; are we alone . . . I mean, are there any aliens?"

Everyone bursts out laughing.

Despite being absolutely famished, having been sitting in the waiting room for hours and not once thinking of food, the councillors do not hurry, as modern society is not only supremely considerate, but it has a soft spot for answering questions. Every adult will put off anything he or she may be doing—that is not a life or death matter—if anyone needs to be answered.

Lenny responds again, "Ah, the question that has perplexed humankind from time immemorial, believe me, Madeleine, it still does.

"We have not encountered any aliens; the generally accepted theory today is that yes, Madeleine, we are alone. Previously, people thought life evolved out of the peculiar conditions on Earth; that is only half true. The genesis and evolution of life is a product of the energy and force of the entire universe; hence, we believe today that the universe, not only Earth, belongs to us and that we have to find a way to make all of it our home, but there is an opposing theory, supported by a sizable minority of people."

"But," intervenes Vaxy, "there is no way of proving this theory; it is one of those theories that cannot be proven, only disproved . . . If you are interested in this topic, Madeleine, all the information is at your fingertips; your PA can help you access all of it. If you still have questions, you can contact anyone of us, anytime, day or night. By the way, I am one of those upholding the heterodox theory alluded to by Lenny." She beams warmly at Madeleine.

"Thank you, everyone; you are all so nice. I am ready to eat now."

They line up at the counter. Brumin hungers for meat, but knows that the moderns are one hundred percent vegan; pity, a succulent rare steak or ribs would have been most welcome! He must admit, like the snacks, the dishes look amazingly scrumptious, if not more so.

The lunch chatter is relaxed. The council members are at pains to not put any pressure on the Adams. There is a lot of merriment. Suddenly, the chatter stops as the councillors become aware of the total relish with which their guests put away their food. They cannot hide their proud smiles; yeah, the food is great; it took humanity a long, long time to produce food that accord one hundred percent with the human body and mind.

Melanie becomes aware of the silence. "Oh, if the food is always this delicious, we will probably all pick up lots of weight!"

Laughter.

"No extra kilos, Melanie, the food does not build any fat, but, in fact, helps the body to maintain a healthy proportion of it," answers Egbert.

"Really? So I do not have to worry about picking up weight? Mom, this is truly a woman's paradise!"

With that, both Madeleine and Melanie dish dollops more of that tasty orangey stew.

Everybody laughs and the chatter hums across the room again. The Adams finish eating some thirty minutes after their hosts, feeling somewhat guilty, but satisfied.

PART TWO

REDIVIVUS!

CHAPTER 8

❖❖❖◈◆◗◐❋◆

Prologue to the Past

Melanie just cannot get used to pouring her heart out to this perfect-looking man . . . who is not a man. They sit at a middle-sized table; his demeanour is very relaxed and amiable, yet empathetic and professional. Her mind drifts. *He is not a man, but a humandroid . . . a super machine . . . thing . . . that looks, moves and speaks just like us . . . .*

Oh my God, I am also not me . . . . neither is the rest of my family . . . . and I am only three weeks old!

The Adams are adapting quite well, except for a problem experienced by Melanie. From the first day, she experienced terrible nightmares in which she relived that awful night. At first, she thought they would pass, but days turned into a week. Lack of sleep took its toll on her and she started to be quite crabby. Her state of mind is delaying her adaptation to her new life. Everything is just too much for her still. She lives in a daze. Her personal medic treated her with aromatherapy and relaxing massages and this helped a little, but, when the problem persisted, PM liaised with her PA and the two agreed to ask Melanie to contact her doctor-scientist, Granville.

Her husband and children were also very worried and encouraged her to listen to PM and PA, which she did. Granville studied her medical file compiled by her personal medic and assessed her himself. It was clear to him that she was reliving the night of their murder over and over; she needed help to get beyond it. He decided that the matter should be handed over to Psychological Services. This is where Fielo comes in, a humandroid attached to the Psychological Services Section. His job is to guide Melanie while she talks about that night in totally safe, protective and emotionally unrestrictive surroundings—for as long as it will take her to come to terms with her past trauma. He sees her every day at her own residence, in a room temporarily fitted for the consultations. After each session, he updates her personal medic and Granville.

Now, Fielo is sitting in his customary chair; Melanie sits opposite him.

The memories rush back like a flooding torrent, almost choking her. She starts shaking. It took four attempts before she could reach this point, and still it remains very difficult.

She vaguely hears Fielo's gentle, husky voice,

"Take your time, Melanie."

It takes a Herculean effort to control herself . . . but she manages to get the words out . . .

"I was . . . I was busy washing the dishes that . . . that night . . ." She could not yet get beyond this point before, but today she will. She owes it to her family and to these amazing people . . . and . . . and . . . things.

CHAPTER 9

Way Back When . . .

H er thoughts stray to her husband as she does the washing up. *He will be tired when he gets home; he has been working late a lot, poor man, just so that we can make ends meet.* Her eyes wander to the clock. Her mind jumps from one thing to the next. She thinks of the neighbour's dog that was found with its head almost severed this morning . . . Yuggh! Who could have done such a thing? Must have been hooligans who roam around at night . . .

She has not been herself for a while. She lost her work over a year ago and, despite looking very hard for another one all this time, she has had no success. Pablo has to carry the entire burden of the maintenance of the family on his shoulders. She has been feeling useless and, whenever she is alone with her thoughts, she mopes over her situation and feels a little sorry for herself. She secretly wonders if Pablo isn't too eager to stay at work as long as possible in order to get away from her melancholic mood swings. The doorbell rings.

"Madeleine! Open for Daddy!"

The key turns with a metallic snap. The door is pushed open with such violence that her heart gives a giant leap. Fear wells up in her bosom, stretches into her throat with steel-like fingers. She can hardly breathe as she mutely stares at this abomination entering their world.

Three young men explode into the house; one immediately shoots Killer as he runs at them. The shooter then storms ahead, into the living room, brandishing his gun. Brumin, who jumped up when the door was pushed open, is smacked across the face with the side of a gun. As the gunman scours through the house, one of his cohorts grabs Madeleine by one arm, pushes a knife against her throat and pushes her into the living room. At the same time, the third one comes right up to her where she still stands frozen and punches her in the face, puts an arm around her neck from behind and pulls her into the living room. "Brumin. Brumin . . ."

"I'm okay, Mom." He sits up and wipes the blood from his cheek with a handkerchief.

Within minutes, they had all three of them sitting on the floor with their hands on their heads.

They quickly stop talking because everyone who doesn't sit still is hit hard across the face or kicked viciously.

Panic seizes her—*Madeleine . . . Brumin!* She never felt so helpless, her children and herself mewling at the mercy of wild-eyed monsters—wielding weapons over them. *Oh God, let my children survive this . . . Let them kill me instead . . .*

The intruders have been mostly quiet the whole time; now, they shout at them. "Where are your wallets, cell phones and bling-bling?"

One kicks Brumin while they shout again, "The money! Where is the money, you shits?"

Then, as if to add weight to his exhortations, he shoots him above his right knee.

Brumin reels with the impact and pain. Madeleine's puling turns into sheer agony. Melanie is frantic.

She must do something to protect them; maybe they still have a chance. "You can get everything we have! My purse is in my bag in the kitchen. My cell phone too."

The children hand over their cell phones. Melanie quickly explains to them where they can get her jewellery. She even refers them to the keys of her car, which is parked in the driveway, without them asking for it. She hopes if they are happy . . . maybe they will stop hurting them—let them live.

The one with the gun stays with them while the other two scour through the house, looking jumpy, eyes popping wildly. It seems like a lifetime before they return with their booty in Brumin's favourite sports bag.

Then the one with the wildest-looking eyes she has ever seen takes the gun from his cohort, gives her a cold smile as he points the barrel between her eyes, and pulls the trigger.

A scream is caught in her throat as her head is rammed backwards. She faintly hears more shots and screams as the very life oozes out of her . . .

In the end, she just blurted it all out. Now she feels exhausted, but relieved. She feels a weight has lifted off her chest, off her mind. Suddenly, she smiles,

"Thanks, Fielo."

She gets up, finds her family in the kitchen and hugs them each with tears rolling down her cheeks.

"I'm here, Mommy's home!"

They all cry . . . except Brumin.

CHAPTER 10

Granville

G ranville relaxes in his garden, enjoying a beverage and some fruit, seeds and nuts while he waits for Fielo's report. He is really concerned about Melanie, but he is confident that she will pull through; the question is: how long will it take?

Granville is still single at twenty-five, firmly built yet slender as he stands six feet tall, which is the average height. He has a rich crop of black hair that he keeps short. He has not yet felt the desire to settle down with someone; maybe, as his mother likes to tell him, he has not yet met the right woman. In any case, his mind is too full of all sorts of matters of learning for him to settle down. He lives alone with his PA, Stan. He studied for four years to become a doctor-scientist, which is a specialist position. He was working in the Merrigold Hospital and the Central Biology Laboratory when the time box was opened. The period immediately following this act is still like a terrible dream to him. He was excited about the scientific prospects held by the box, but, sadly he lost one friend and a cousin in the ensuing cataclysm.

He felt honoured and excited when he was asked by the Council of the Realm to be part of the regeneration team. Being part of the team has been a truly unique experience, regenerating life and bringing it across millennia. He remembers how elated he was when the patients awoke—it was surreal and exotic woven into one.

The tone of his wrist communicator brings him out of his reverie. It is a message from Fielo. The report has been sent to his digital portal. He moves to his study to read the report on his computer, not being in the mood to read it in hologram format.

It is a tremendous struggle for him to read the section of the report that summarises the events of that fateful night, having to stop reading and look away from the text after every sentence. After reading the report, he sits with his face in his hands. This poor family really went through a terrible ordeal. "Stan," he calls into his wrist. "Can you come here, please?"

He motions to Stan to sit on the chair that he has occupied on so many occasions when he, Granville, needed a sounding board.

"Read this, then let me pick your brain a little."

"Done."

"You know, Stan, I have learnt a lot about the violence of one person upon another since we opened the time box. I underwent counselling, as well, but reading how this incident actually unfolded and how it affected people while they were still in the situation, people I now know, makes it hard for me to develop a proper understanding of it all. There is something I don't get. It is as if my mind has been dragged back to the time of the Adam family and it also suffers from the reality of murder. How can history be so powerful? I don't know if you understand what I mean . . ."

"I do, Granville. The reality and, in fact, the presence of murder has jumped thousands of years to re-embed itself in the psyche of modern humans. It is too late to close Pandora's Box, though."

"I know, Stan. I am also of a mind that the horrible presence cannot be removed for generations, but we have to develop this knowledge into constructive channels and prevent it from affecting us further psychologically. Can you imagine how Melanie, Madeleine and Brumin must have felt in those perilous moments? I am just very happy that Melanie is the only one struggling to overcome this trauma."

"Can we really be sure she is the only one?"

Granville reflects for a moment. "Good question . . . Only time will tell . . . I also think of the murderers; they were humans too. What went on in their minds throughout that episode? Did they not feel the Adams' fear, their pain? How did they feel when the Adams' lay there, in their own house, dead at their hands? Could material things alone have caused them to act so extremely contrary to human nature and the human spirit? I feel that I am missing something, Stan."

"We all are, for, despite all the knowledge we can generate about the past, the past will remain alien to us, as we cannot place ourselves in the minds of other living beings. No epoch can be properly judged outside of its time, because the human mind— that does the judging—changes too much. The Adam family can, however, add a lot of light on the subject, provided the modern mind is capable of developing an understanding of the complexities of the peri-primitive mind."

"I get what you are saying, but if I extend it logically, it means that we cannot really judge the murderers! We can only try to understand. Are they themselves victims of their age? Why did they look for valuables—why did they not have what they needed? Their descriptions of being wild-eyed could mean that they were sick or drugged; if drugged, why did they take them, who gave it to them and would that mean they were responsible for their actions? We can only become what is created by society. In murdering, they become dehumanised; can I be justified to say this is perhaps a worse fate than that which befell their victims? For their victims lost their lives, but in the end everybody dies, yet it is what you die as that is more important than the fact of dying itself."

"At a certain level, you would be justified, but the matter is complex. It is easy to blame individuals, for, after society punishes them—like was done in the past—society feels it has dealt with the problem and moves on, but the cause of the problem has not been resolved and the scene is set for repetition ad infinitum. This is not to say that adults are not responsible for their deeds; the point is that the buck does not stop with the perpetrator, but with society."

"I think you are right, Stan. Thank you. I do appreciate your support. So, for the moment, Melanie just needs time to work through and come to terms with her experience and the consultations must continue. We both then concur with Fielo's view? I will also recommend to the Council of the Realm that a project be developed to help us all understand exactly why and how humans could be driven to murder, how it was possible for people to become so depraved, so un-human."

"That is a good idea, Granville, and I also enjoyed our conversation."

————•┅═╍•❀❁◐◑◓❁❀•╍═┅•————

CHAPTER 11

Pablo's Secret

Melanie has been asleep for hours. Nowadays, her sleep is very peaceful. Pablo wishes he can sleep as soundly, but something has been troubling him since day one of his new life, preying on his mind. He sits up in bed and looks at his lovely wife's sleeping face, her sleeping hair. Gazing at her face, his heart feels as warm as an evening glow. He looks at the rich and supple swarthy skin, the high cheekbones, the friendly lines at the side of her eyes and at the corners of her mouth . . . the full lips. He listens to her gentle breathing and it is all like music to his ears and eyes, for he loves her with all his heart. How beautiful she is; at forty-five years of age, she can easily pass for thirty-five, thanks to her good genes, but also to the regeneration process, as well as the contented life she is now leading. He strokes her soft hair, then her cheek, then her lips—the latter causes his fingertips to tingle sharply, leading to a quivering sensation in his lips that could only be stilled by a tender kiss. She smiles in her sleep as his lips brush over hers. But, when that did not help his demanding lips, he did it again, taking his time.

He lies on his back with his eyes closed, reflects and smiles. He always thought he was just plain lucky that such a gorgeous beauty would even give him a second glance, let alone marry him! He never thought of himself as much of a looker—not that it bothered him, not at all. Not really of muscular built, a little on the short side—Melanie liked to tease him that she was taller than him—round cheeks, a beard that grows too fast, pleasant-looking deep brown eyes, and a forehead that frowns quite a lot.

The smile fades . . . he drifts off to a joyless sleep . . . .

He finds himself in a mall full of people, alone, then he sees his family, he calls them. They do not hear him and he rushes to them. He speaks to his wife, she gives him a horrible look, turns and walks away with the children in tow, each of whom looks back at him accusingly, turns away and follows their mom. He stands alone, dejected, heart-broken, and he wakes up with all this sorrow sitting on his chest.

For about a year, he was unfaithful to his wife; sometimes he was really working late, but other times he was with one of his mistresses—like that night it all ended. There was Susan and . . . and . . . the other one.

It started at work. He always admired Susan, but he kept his distance as any decent married man should; she was hot and vivacious and she liked to flirt with him. But, after a while, after he gave up on his wife, he allowed the flirtation to develop into a steamy affair. This transgression seemed to open a door somewhere in his psyche that led to a place where he could dress himself up in and live a lie. While seeing Susan, he started a relationship with Petra, a woman he met when he offered her a lift one day when she was waiting for a bus in the rain. When he was with his mistresses, he temporarily forgot the sorrow he felt so deeply when he was with his wife, who seemed to live in a bubble that was just all about herself. She was constantly self-centred, moody and negative. So defensive that discussions between them dried up a long time ago, as everything ended up being about her or her insecurities. Only small talk and 'official family business' survived. Even if she did something for the children, it was actually about making herself feel good, like spoiling Brumin; if spoiling a child is never good for the child, why is it then really being done—to make the spoiler feel good for some twisted reason that can be found if one digs into the spoiler's childhood or adult relationships. Reason gave way to emotionalism and, as time went by, her very personality became eroded as if for lack of maintenance. His wife stagnated as a person, became an empty shell, a realisation that hurt him immeasurably, for he felt that he had lost a partner and that he was married to something that was somewhere between a valued artefact and a pet. And he allowed his disappointment to change him too; he became a deceitful person, a notion he has always abhorred.

When he was with his mistresses, he was on top of the world. They were free, and that liberated him. But now his past betrayal nags him. Is it guilt, because, had he been home earlier that night, he might probably have been able to prevent the tragedy? Or is it because he does not really feel responsible for what Pablo did—he certainly feels a duality in his personality.

On the one hand, he is Pablo; on the other, he feels like someone else in Pablo's head and body—yet the one feels a tremendous loyalty to the other. He already wanted to open up to Melanie, but he sensed that the time was not right, until now.

"Mel. Mel . . ." He cannot wait any longer.

He nudges her lightly.

"Hmmm?" Slowly and languidly, she opens her eyes. "Can't you sleep?"

She closes her eyes again, fast asleep.

"Hey, open your eyes . . ."

He kisses her on her eyes.

She sits up. "Okay, I'm awake . . . give me a minute."

She nestles up against him.

"I have to speak to you, and no, it cannot wait."

She sits up after about five minutes, rubbing her bleary eyes and yawning.

"For about a year, I had affairs. It started at work . . ."

She puts her finger on his mouth.

"Shhhh . . . don't let it keep you awake at night; it wasn't really you, was it? And I'm not really me, am I?"

A dry laugh emits from his throat. "And here I was having nightmares since the day I was reborn! But seriously, Mel, I feel bad about it. It pains me to think that I could have done something like that because I know I always loved you, deeply."

"Pabbie, I love you too, but if you ever cheat on me, I will ask PA to cut your balls off! By the way, the real Melanie was seeing one of the neighbours; I'm not saying who."

They both laugh heartily and Pablo finds it amazing that he does not feel jealous in the least.

"I am supposed to feel jealous, but I am not because I know it wasn't really you. We were quite a messed up family, weren't we, Mel?"

"I am sorry, Pablo. I know I had a lot to do with what went wrong. I just could not pull myself together since I lost my job. It was as if some negative fog clouded my brain and from there seeped into every ounce of my being. I am really sorry. What I do know is that I always loved you immensely. I was only joking about the neighbour. I would never betray you, though I did not give you the life you deserved. But I will make up for it, I promise, even if I am seven thousand years late." She kisses him tenderly and lies against him with both her arms around him.

"Tell me about it . . . maybe we can both learn from it."

"I cannot say how exactly it started. This woman, Susan—at work—always flirted with me, but I ignored it for a long time. Then there was another woman . . . Petra; I think I met her when I gave her a lift . . . The truth is, they made me forget the difficulties I had at home. I know there is no excuse and I am not making any; can you understand what I mean if I say I'm actually glad I'm not living that life anymore? I promise I will never betray you again."

"Pabbie, how do you feel about yourself, I mean as a person . . . being a clone? As for me, I really feel great. I feel that I am Melanie, yet I also am not. More like someone else—brand new—inhabiting Melanie's body and mind. It's like Melanie is the wool with which I knit, but the jersey is all new . . . I promise you, if this was not the case, I would have asked PA how do I go about divorcing you!"

They laugh.

"You put it so well, it is exactly how I feel. I feel sorry for what Pablo did and I do feel responsible, but not completely. I certainly feel I am Pablo, but starting out with a clean slate. After all, I have ninety-five percent of his personality! I was afraid of how you would respond, but I am so glad that you are taking my infidelities so well. You truly are the best. I want to make the best of my new life. I want to continue all the good things Pablo did, but I want to do better than he did and I want to show you and the kids how much I really love you and I want to become a modern man and a real asset to this noble society. Mel, I love you much more than I ever did before."

They melt into a long, passionate kiss.

"You know, Pabbie, we have the best of both worlds literally! I agree, let us make the best of it. And for my part, I accept that I am Melanie!"

"Pleased to meet you, Melanie. I am Pablo!"

And so they continue talking throughout the night and everything between them feels so different and so fresh. It is as if their true selves emerged from the shells of Melanie and Pablo and they find themselves in bed—two liberated souls together—for the first time.

When PM opens the curtains ever so slightly at the pre-set time, the early sunrays find them tightly woven in each other's arms and smile as they play on their faces. PM holds her breath, for she does not want them to wake just yet.

CHAPTER 12

⊷≕❖⊰⊙⊙⊱❖≕⊶

Settling In

D uring the first few days, Brumin explores the house over and over; we catch him on day three. His firm, shortish muscular frame moves casually through their residence as if he is on a visit to a museum. All in all, he is a good-looking young man, with short dark hair, dark eyes, bushy eyebrows and a strong chin. Overall, his face gives the impression of inner strength. For such a young man, he certainly has a lot of deep frown lines on his forehead. An indication of his semi-morose disposition. Yes, Brumin does not laugh much. But today, he is as happy as a fly on a pie.

Brumin cannot believe the spacious accommodation that was now *their* house. His bedroom, huge, of course, has its own bathroom and adjoining study, which is fitted with a magnificent computer workstation on a huge work desk—that looks more like an oversized, old-fashioned escritoire. Two walls are covered with as yet empty bookshelves. He makes a mental note—PA showed him how to order books from the library—he better get to it, but first he needs to finalise what he is going to study. He looks at the computer again and does not know what to think. It is only a keyboard! He touches a key, and a screen with a pleasant face issues immediately from a tiny nozzle. He goes back to the bedroom.

The bed is, in fact, 'alive' in a way, and feels like soft, inviting velvet. The mattress moves while you lie on it to support your body in the best possible ways. It is built into a sort of micro-hospital called the personal medic or PM for short. One wall makes way for the array of exquisite walk-in cupboards made of the grandest wood he could ever imagine. Washing machines are a thing of the past, with the cupboards automatically cleaning their contents as the need arises. Two walls inside the bedroom look like tough old-fashioned television screens, which can be decorated with colours, images, videos or text using the computer.

The basement is fitted with a sizable gymnasium with exotic machines, and leads to a huge, splendiferous pool that appears to be fed by a small waterfall at the far end, which, in reality, is merely a phase in the circulation of the pool's water! He looks for Perell, the *spirituel* humandroid who takes care of the basement facilities and who doubles up as the gym instructor and pool guard. But Perell finds him.

"Good morning, Brumin; how are you today?"

"Fine, Perell, I am cool. Just looking around; I will come for a workout and a swim later."

"That is just fine, Brumin. I shall be waiting."

Then there is the incredible media room, with its magical media unit or media centre, which is twice the size of his bedroom. The television he was used to, made way over thousands of years for a composite media centre—which is a small golf ball-sized magical nozzle, made of some intricate metal-crystal compound. The nozzle, in fact, contains thousands of micro-machines, which, together, create all the splendour of the media centre. The unit is activated and controlled by voice prompting or mind impulses, but a remote control device can also be used. Once it is activated, it automatically spews out a screen, the size of which can be altered at command. The amazing thing about the screen is that it looks like a translucent bubble, and projects three-dimensional images and holograms. Apart from functioning as a television, the media centre is also a telephone, internet unit, radio, music centre, digital education unit, and above all, it links with Council Control and all relevant databases in the world. Unlike in his era, the internet is not based on websites, but temporary websites are created for users based on their requests. Unfortunately, the Adams cannot yet manage to control the centre with mind impulses. In the media room, there are four very cosy couches, a few lounge chairs, four coffee tables and a beverage bar built into one of the walls. The walls are bare and the two large windows are covered with blinds. Brumin moves softly across the plush carpet to the kitchen.

The huge kitchen, with its beautiful, sleek, black, shiny rectangular table made of a material unknown to him—a type of metallic wood—is in the middle of the kitchen, surrounded by ten comfortable chairs. It is fitted with shiny, semi-transparent ceramic cupboards, a refrigeration corner that looks like a large ordinary cupboard, a media nozzle and a beverage bar. If you push the right button, your drink slides out of the wall within seconds! All you have to do is rinse your glass or cup afterwards and place it in its proper slot in the wall. PA explained that kitchens are more like nostalgic entertainment areas, as food is prepared in restaurants and delivered to houses, but on occasion families make their own food for fun. The restaurants are also closed three times a year when all families participate in cooking competitions so that the culture of home-based food making is not lost. Winning new foods and drinks are incorporated into the menus of the restaurants. Brumin smiles when he remembers his mother's reaction. "Aw . . . no shopping!"

The living room is the coolest in the house—it has the most beautiful thick carpet he has ever seen, the plushest couches, beautifully festooned coffee tables and all sorts of interesting objects. Unlike the bedrooms, it has old-fashioned paintings and triptychs on walls that look normal to Brumin. To the side of the room is a special chess table fitted with a built-in chess board and timer—chess being the most popular sport worldwide. He finds it interesting that there was no media unit, supposedly to encourage family communication.

Each house has a power unit that levitates on top of a metre-long pedestal that extends from the roof. It is spherical and looks like a softly glowing prickly pear the size of a soccer ball and slowly rotates at one-hundredth the speed of the Earth, but in the opposite direction. It is an awesome sight, and all the Adams enjoy standing on the roof just to simply look at it as it glows a faint blue, the tips of its numerous porcupine-like bristles blinking in more colours than he knew existed. The sphere expands and contracts rhythmically, as if it is breathing. The unit is, in fact, a tiny, but powerful, generator that uses sunlight and many other cosmic energy rays that strike the Earth, and transforms them into electrical energy. It constantly maintains a reserve that can last three months. He smiles when he thinks of how he tried to figure out where the light bulbs were hidden! Light bulbs are a thing of the past! Electrical light is no longer a by-product of heat; it is created in its own glory—issuing from the walls or ceilings themselves.

There can be no denying it—he is happy here; his whole family is happy here.

Despite Melanie's troubles, the first week is like a dream for the Adams. The family was asked to not go beyond their garden for one week, giving them time to find themselves, learn whatever they need to know about the workings of society and to adjust psychologically to their new lives. This orientation week was regarded as necessary if they were not to be overwhelmed by what was awaiting them on the outside. To their PAs fell the task to ensure that each was as prepared as possible.

For the entire week, the Adams house has the atmosphere of a classroom. There are discussions upon discussions. One-on-ones with the PAs; plenary sessions. Exploring the A to Z of life by means of the digital education unit and the internet. Every Adam wonders if his or her brain power was enhanced, for they are just absorbing it all like ever-thirsty sponges. The most difficult part for everyone is to not be able to go out there and see the things they are learning about. Though Brumin burns to see the sky-hoppers, and even go sky-hopping himself, he is afraid to go into the garden the first day, but cannot contain his curiosity the second.

As Melanie listens to Vida answering some of Madeleine's questions in the media room, a tightness clasps her chest. "Vida," she cries. "Please tell me shopping is not a relic of the past!"

"No, no, Melanie, only changed in form . . . Let me show you. Name a topic to shop . . ."

"Clothes," the answer comes back immediately.

"All right, shopping channel, female clothes."

A new screen forms out of the big screen and moves right in front of them.

"Show me all the blouses for my size."

The screen envelopes Vida, who pulls Melanie in, who is treated to the greatest shopping experience in history.

"End."

The shopping screen disappears.

"If you want something, you touch it and state order and you will receive it in one hour."

"Nice . . ." is all Melanie can get out.

"All modern clothes are made of mixtures of natural and synthetic materials. We call them intelligent because they have loads of micro-computers in them. They all come in single sheets with a hole for the head or feet, once you stick your head or feet through, the sheet adjusts and transforms itself. And look, if you squeeze the cloth between two fingers . . . like this . . . you see, a mini screen emerges, allowing you to change the design!"

"Lovely! I always wanted to design my own clothes! And the shoes?"

"They are all made of special soles that emit electrons that form the upper parts."

"Okay, Vida, thanks; I think I will go on a shopping spree tonight!"

Day two. They all venture into the garden together. They saw images of the neighbourhood on the internet, but nothing beats the real thing.

They have the most beautiful garden any one of them has ever seen—flowers of all shapes and colours, big and small plants, water features, rockeries with unfamiliar rocks, a few benches and numerous colourful butterflies, ladybirds and birds visiting the trees and chirping away merrily. The far edge of the garden is lined with an assortment of low fruit trees and the two sides are demarcated by a combination of bird baths and waist-high shrubs and papaveraceous plants.

Apart from the trees and bird baths, there is no fence around the house and they do not see burglar bars anywhere. They look at the houses around them, and strain their eyes to catch a glimpse of the house art. They cannot see much, as the spaces between houses are obscured by trees everywhere. No roads, only lanes for walking. Despite the exceptional technology, everything they cast their eyes on looks extremely natural, except the walls of the houses and the few travellors they see floating by in the distance. The PAs are with them, in case they may have any questions.

"Boris, why do we not see any sky-hoppers or any of the neighbours?"

"Everyone was asked to give you space, especially for this week, Brumin, but there is one going, if you look between those two houses—oops, he's gone, sorry."

"What is that in the distance . . . over there . . . looking like a triangle?"

Vida replies, "It's the top of a pyramid. Every region has a couple of pyramids. These are final resting places of the deceased. People who die are cremated, then their ashes are mixed with a substance and compressed into a diamond. These are given space on the outer and inside walls of pyramids, with plaques dedicated to each. Family and friends may visit the pyramids to be in the presence of their loved ones . . ."

Just then, they hear a little boy shrieking with delight coming in their direction, with probably his mom running after him—or is it a humandroid? "Come back here, Ikey!"

Too late. He appears right in front of them. Ikey is about four years old; he has shorts on, and that is all. His cheeks, forehead and upper body are smeared with streaks of mud. His shorts and feet are as dirty as can be. "Hello, you must be the Adams . . ." He proffers Brumin a dirty hand.

They are all too perplexed to get a word in before his mom gets to him. An exotic and fresh-looking woman in her thirties, with face flustered, dressed in a dungaree with bare, muddy feet, comes past the birdbaths, grabs him by the arm and hits him once, hard on his behind.

"That is for not listening. Now you go back to the house and wait for me. I am not done with you, little man!"

Ikey runs home wailing, straight to their PA to complain about his mother. The perplexity of the Adams just grows. *They hit their children,* thinks Melanie. *Even I did not do that anymore.*

What a dirty tyke, thinks Brumin. *He must have been really enjoying whatever he was doing.* They are brought out of their thoughts by their neighbour.

"I am so sorry you had to meet your neighbours in this way, but parenthood does not have a special time allocation," she says with laughter.

"My name is Chelle, my son is Ikey. He is a real terror—be forewarned! Once you have settled in, my beloved and I would like to invite you over for dinner, but not to worry, we will give you fair warning. Sorry that I look like this; I was busy teaching Ikey about the properties of sand when he just ran off. I did not expect to make your acquaintance just yet."

She shakes hands with everybody as they introduce themselves.

"Chelle," says Melanie, speaking for the whole family. "It is a real pleasure to meet you. We look forward to your invitation."

She leaves them with a wave and a smile, and Brumin secretly hopes she whacks Dirty Ikey some more!

"What a nice lady and boy."

"Yes, love, especially the boy; can you believe what you just saw?"

Pablo shakes his head. Everybody laughs and they continue exploring with their eyes and ears. They hear birds twitter; two visit one of their birdbaths, the sun is shining and there is not a cloud in the sky and all around them they get a sense of total tranquillity. They inspect the flowers. They walk around the house. The outside walls have a metallic yet glassy veneer that is, in fact, a rudimentary computer screen, rudimentary not in its technology, but because of its limited functionality. It is limited to displaying colours, pictures, video and text.

"PA, the surroundings are like a true paradise—so peaceful . . ."

"Yes, Melanie, quite salubrious."

"These walls are very interesting, PA; what are they made of?"

"They are made of an alloy of marint and grandax from Mars, Pablo, manufactured with a little vaNadzum and white sand and numerous chemicals. Would you like the names of the chemicals?"

"No, PA . . . it looks like a tough television screen, but with a metallic underside. Mars, you say; quite extraordinary, PA."

"Yes, Pablo, and unbreakable."

They end up in the garden again, sit on the benches and discuss the house art they will use. It is agreed that everyone will get a chance to decide and program the house art for a period of two weeks. As mother of the house, Melanie gets the first opportunity.

They end up spending many hours in the garden, mainly sitting on the benches and chatting, only going back inside when the twilight breeze reminds them of the temperature-controlled warmth inside.

Day seven. The councillors who inaugurated them into their new lives are guests at their house. The PAs arranged for a moderate lunch, which is enjoyed outside, in the garden. This was a courtesy call and this time around the Adams are quite free with the councillors, who have the aura of pleasant uncles and aunts around them. Yes, they affirm that they are most happy here. Yes, they have received a great induction from the PAs. And, while Pablo was still thanking the councillors and all the people of the world for this wonderful second life in this wonderful society, Dirty Ikey suddenly pushes his smudgy face through the leaves of a brush.

"Hello! Hello! How are you?"

Gerry answers him, "We are all very happy and fine, young man; what is your name?"

"Ikey! What is yours, Uncle?"

"I'm Uncle Gerry, come sit here beside me and I will ask your mom if you may have lunch with us."

Ikey is only too eager.

"And tell Mommy, Uncle Gerry, she mustn't hit me anymore."

They all laugh. Gerry proceeds to introduce everyone to Ikey.

"You should know, Ikey, we men always listen to the women; you should try listening to your mom, then things will work out better for you."

Just then, his mother is on the scene, but Gerry respectfully mollifies her and she leaves Ikey with them for lunch. She declines to join the lunch herself and leaves only after Gerry promises he will clean her little angel before the meal.

As soon as his mother is out of earshot, Ikey whispers in Gerry's ear that he wants to ask something.

"Sure, Ikey, go ahead."

"Uncle Gerry, did people from the past drink milk from the cow's titties?"

The laughter was uneasy, embarrassed, but Brumin seethed with anger! *The bloody dirty tyke!*

"No, Ikey . . . ." replied Gerry. "Not like that. If you lived in the past, my boy, you would also have drunk cow's milk. But the milk was first taken out of the cows, then it was made safe for humans, then it was put in bottles or made into powders and only then was it used by people."

Vaxy chimes in, "Ikey, milk is a very good source of many elements needed by the body, and you know what, especially children needed a lot of it. So if you lived in the past, you would have loved drinking cows' milk."

"Yuuuuuuk! I would have drunk only water, Aunty!"

They can just laugh, until Lenny manages to change the subject.

Over lunch, the councillors explain to the Adams about the monument in commemoration of all the innocent lives lost due to human deeds throughout the ages and invite the family to the inauguration and opening of the monument, named the House of Primitive Human Brutality.

They also inform the Adams that a lot of people from around the world want to communicate with them, and, if it is in order with all of them, Council Control will open a dedicated broadcast channel through which people can say hi and ask them basic questions. As this could take up a lot of their time, the channel will operate only for one week and their PAs will act as their secretaries, summarising all incoming messages and answering them as per their instructions. Everyone agrees excitedly.

Now that their orientation is over, they should slot into society like everybody else, but the council will always keep special tabs on their well-being. When they depart, the councillors hug each of them and everyone of them picks Ikey up and, in a nice way, asks him to listen to his mother. He says he will, but Brumin does not believe him, as he sees the glint of boredom in his tiny devilish eyes as he pretends to be all ears.

Week two comes and goes like a tornado. Different councillors pick them up in the mornings and take them sightseeing far and wide and every evening they spend answering their mail. The Adams find the trips breathtaking; never could they imagine that the world would ever be such a beautiful place. At one point, Pablo muses that a life of peregrination in this world would be like wandering through paradise.

They answer thousands of messages each, and they simply love all the attention. Most people only introduce themselves, stating where they live, and wishing them a wonderful life. Only a few ask basic questions, but not one question is about their previous lives.

CHAPTER 13

———— • ❦ ❦ • ————

Worldwide Theme:
CENTURY 20-21

O ne interesting matter that the councillors left the
Adams with is the worldwide theme: Century
20-21. The family is sitting with the PAs in the
kitchen, one of whom is busy re-explaining it to them. Whenever
a situation of immense significance affects society as a whole, even
a major achievement in any field, a worldwide theme is declared by
the Council of the Realm, as has now been done.

Madeleine interrupts, "Sorry, sorry to interrupt, but you know
what will really help me understand how this works—if I know
how the educational system works. Can you put that in context for
me, Sipho?"

"Of course, Madeleine; I will try to be pithy . . ." Sipho takes
them on a journey that makes their eyes light up with wonder.

"All people, from the day they are born till the day they die,
are part of the education system. In the first four years, education
is informal—conducted by both parents under the supervision
of the PA—this process is called Mom-Dad Schools. Moms and
dads are responsible for teaching their children the basic skills of
mathematics, reading, writing, basic artistic skills, chess, manners
and ethics.

"The next ten years are spent in schools, facilitated by humandroids, who are supervised by professors, all of whom are human. In these schools, the main foci of learning are mathematics, nature, social studies and language. All students from the age of five also attend a school of sports and arts. The following six years are taken up by tertiary studies, which are centred on higher level skills and knowledge and includes one year of space travel study.

"Thereafter, education takes two forms: work-based training and research. After the period of tertiary study, each person becomes a spoke in the wheels of society. He or she will spend three hours a day working and three hours on work-related study, five days a week, excluding holidays. Upon completion of a work study course, a citizen continues in the position for a further one year before moving on to a different field—as versatility is highly prescribed by society.

"At the age of twenty-two, a citizen may apply to become a specialist in any field and, at the age of thirty, a citizen may request to be appointed as a professor. Professors train and guide students as well as humandroid-teachers and parent-teachers, and, while they do this, they study to become philosophers.

"A philosopher first grade is a connoisseur of mathematics and natural science. A philosopher second grade is a connoisseur of thought, mathematics and natural science. A philosopher third grade is a connoisseur of thought, mathematics, natural science and the social sciences. A philosopher fourth grade has the same qualifications as the previous one, but is also a connoisseur of life. All philosophers fourth grade determine their own research and may form or join research groups. People normally participate in research groups until their lives come to an end.

"The schools and tertiary institutions are co-ordinated by the Education Department, travel study is co-ordinated by the Youth University, work-based studies by the various academies linked to the various sectors of the economy, the professors are determined and co-ordinated by the Council of Teachers and philosopher training is co-ordinated by the Council of Philosophers."

Madeleine wanted to know more about the space travel study programme.

Boris explained, "By roughly the age of nineteen, all youth are expected to have completed at least one year in this programme. One choice is travelling to one or more of the galactic destinations where they would study the environment, life and industries existing there. The other choice includes a journey without a destination to study phenomena in space; in this case, all the studying takes place on board the space travellor."

Brumin stops rubbing his leg. "How many space destinations are there and the space travellors must be huge?"

Boris switches the media screen on and shows them live images of the various destinations and of a few space travellors.

"There are fifty-three space destinations all over the galaxy; they are all manned by humandroids only, with people visiting for studying purposes and to make ongoing assessments. Through your media screens, you can communicate directly with the control at each destination, as well as with the control of every space travellor on a study journey." He continues to show them how to initiate the communications.

"Worldwide theme, Century 20-21, has the following aspects. Every researcher will spend one quarter of her/his study time researching any topic with respect to the 20th and 21st centuries.

"In every school and tertiary institution, one quarter of the study time will be used to learn about any topics pertaining to those centuries.

Data Centre will update all PAs and other humandroids fulfilling educational and cultural roles with all available information on the chosen era.

"A special media channel—Channel Century 20-21—has been created, on which all people will publish their work, questions, replies and comments.

Century 20-21 Control has already been created. It will interface with all the relevant bodies and will supervise the implementation of the worldwide theme, it will manage the channel and it will ensure veracity of whatever is produced."

Throughout the entire explanation, the Adams are mostly absolutely quiet, everyone afraid they might spoil the beauty of the pearls dropping from the PA's lips. Then a smile flashes across Madeleine's face, "I know what we can do . . . what about each of us writing something that we know about and share it with everybody? I mean, what can be better than a take on our time by people coming from that time? Come on . . . come on . . . what do you say?"

"Mmmmm . . . not a bad idea . . . then why don't we all write something that shows the positive side of our world. Ok, I am in, but let us discuss what we will be writing about. I will write about . . . let me see, I got it: the joys of motherhood in the 21st century."

"Are you sure Mom, you said positive . . . ." Melanie was caught off-guard.

"What do you mean, Brumin, how was motherhood not positive?"

"I'm just thinking Mom, how many moms had to struggle on their own while the fathers were not around or just leaving caring for the kids to the mothers? Even Dad, right Dad . . . even you . . . I remember with Madeleine, if she cried, you called Mom and handed her over!"

"True, Son, I remember that. You make a good point . . . isn't it so, Mel?"

"True, but even so, I will focus on the positive aspects—we do not always have to be so serious and only see the dark side of things."

Madeleine cuts in with her usual excuberance, "I can write about being a teenager!"

Brumin just laughs, causing her to sulk.

"Ok, I get it, I will write about . . . the high buildings we had as I see that all buildings here—except those pyramids—are not higher than one-story."

"Good choice, Madeleine, I will write about the artistic expressions of the great artists of our time, and you Brumin?"

"I will write about the popular movies for people of my age."

Melanie gives him a smile, "That was a very constructive Adam-family meeting! Well done guys . . ." And everyone started to talk at the same time . . .

CHAPTER 14

Pablo and Melanie

Pablo and Melanie are sitting at a restaurant on top of Table Mountain enjoying a cocktail.

"Pabbie, when we started to go out, you did show a romantic side, but, after about six months, that seemed to dry up. This past week, you have just blown me away. Thanks, Love, I cannot put into words how much I have enjoyed these past few days. What are we doing after today?"

"Tomorrow, we will go sky-hopping with the Franks—they will teach us. The day after, we will go for a picnic in Paris and we will spend the weekend at a Black Sea resort. You know, Mel . . ." He gazes deep into her eyes. ". . . I have also been enjoying our time together tremendously." He grabs her free hand; she squeezes his and smiles.

"I promise, this time I will not last for six months; this is for keeps. I would like us to spend a lot of special time together; once we start working, we can maybe work out some sort of plan?"

"Good idea, my husband, we must also work into that plan quality family time. In the past, we did not spend enough time together as a family. Now, there are so many things we can do together."

"Yes, let's do that, and by the way, do you know what I enjoy most here . . . in the future?"

"Of course I know." She laughs. "The travellors!"

"How did you . . . ? Never mind . . . Never in my wildest dreams could I imagine that the cars of the future would be so amazing, but enough of that." He takes her hand again. "Did I tell you recently that I love you with all my heart?"

"Only about an hour ago . . ."

"You know what adds greatly to my pleasure, Mel, is the fact that visas are no longer required—the world is at last truly united."

"Yes, isn't that just the grandest of things? No more posturing between countries, no more 'my country is better than yours' or 'you are third world . . . we are first world' . . . I just love it, Pabbie, and you know what is just as wonderful? It seems that the Chinese no longer live in China and the Indians no longer in India; I mean, everyone just lives in the world!"

Pablo laughs. "And it seems like this is the way it has always been."

Both laugh heartily. "But we know better, hey Pabbie?"

"Yeah, sweetheart, we know better . . ."

"Pabbie . . . I want to visit Antarctica soon . . ."

"But we were there just last week!"

"I know, but I loved it so much, the greenery, the waterfalls, the animals, the ocean . . ."

"Sure, love, no problem . . ."

Pablo and Melanie have reinvigorated their love for each other. They have both changed—they are both free of spirit, happy, outgoing, relaxed and have a renewed zest for life. All the chips of old have disappeared from their shoulders.

Melanie smiled when she first noticed how Pablo looks at travellors and it was she who told him to learn how to pilot, which, by the way, even a toddler can do. She secretly thinks they are always visiting faraway places just so that he can enjoy flying these beautiful creations around, but she just loves that he is having such a great time, as happy as a lark behind the pilot's gadgets.

As they fly home, Melanie falls asleep with her head on Pablo's leg. A warm feeling comes over him and tears rush to his eyes. He laughs. *What's with this maudlin gush?* Then he looks at her again; she is also serenely smiling, with her eyes closed. He does not want to be anywhere else right now. He thinks of the first time he saw her; she had a loose-fitting white slacks suit-thing on; wow, she looked so divine—like life itself! He knew then that if he did not marry this woman, his life would no longer have any meaning.

His mind flits to when he saw a real travellor the first time—it was flying low over the house; what a sight it was to behold! It was early evening and all its lights were sparkling—green, red, amber, pink, blue, gold and white—he looked and looked until Melanie told him he could blink again because it was gone!

Travellors are civilian transportation vehicles and there are two kinds: space roamers and commuters. A commuter is what is used for everyday travel and is roughly the size of two small buses next to each other. Pristine, like a baby's eyes, it is shaped like a diamond that sits on a spherical disc—that contains the two engines. They come in only one colour—a deep, deep charcoal that seems as if it can swallow you whole.

A wheel-less machine, a travellor never touches the ground and its engines make a very soft whirring sound. Inside, it has a large cockpit in the front that can seat two passengers plus the pilot. Behind the seats, there is a bathroom with a toilet to the side, beyond which is a huge lounge, which has a media unit, bookshelf, beverage bar, food unit for storing meals and snacks, and six comfortable seats. Space roamers, on the other hand, are much bigger and come in different sizes.

The cockpit is fitted with an array of gadgets and the steering is done by means of a large ball that is moved in the direction the pilot wants it to go. Pilots are not really necessary, as these ships of the skies are fitted with excellent auto-pilots. The vehicles also respond to voice commands. The power unit is similar to that of a house and is situated right on top of the diamond.

To get a travellor is the easiest thing in the world. His PA ordered one for him and it was delivered within ten minutes. He can return it whenever he wants or just keep it for at most a month, as routine maintenance is done monthly. If he suddenly gets hungry, he just orders a meal and it is delivered to him in flight anywhere in the world.

The ride home was just too short for him.

"Mel . . . Mel . . . we are home . . . I have a surprise for you . . ."

She lifts her head, stretches and rubs her eyes, "Whaaat?"

"We have to wake up early tomorrow, I arranged a very special trip for us—it will take a week—so put in what you need, I arranged for clothes and food . . . we will leave at 7:00."

"Okay, Mr. Full-of-Surprises, I will be ready . . . I suppose I will have to wait until tomorrow to find out where you will be taking me. I'm tired, I'm going to sleep now. You coming?"

They are finishing their breakfast when one of the PAs informs them that their travellor has arrived. They hastily go outside with their bags, with Melanie in front. Outside the door they are taken aback.

"This must be a space travellor! You did not tell me we are going into space! Lordie! Pabbie—you are crazy . . . words just dry up."

Pablo grins, this is the first time he sees a space travellor. It is the size of ten commuter travellors. The pilot meets them, "Good Morning, my name is Bernie, I will be your pilot and guide. Step aboard please, whenever you are ready."

They greet him and enter. He shows them around and they absorb everything in total silence. The cockpit has place for five people and is fitted with a multitude of fancy, blinking gadgets. The living quarters are extremely comfortable—two bathrooms, a huge lounge, two studies, three bedrooms, one gym, two big activity rooms and one command centre. An entire section is devoted to food and drink—which is fully automated. Meals are made at the press of a button—or the issuing of a voice command. They find more than enough space outfits in the main bedroom.

"Now, before we depart, is there anything you may need?"

"No, Bernie, we are ready and eager to go! Let's lift off!" Pablo is certainly in a happy mood.

They make themselves comfortable in the lounge as they leave Mother Earth.

"Now, Pabbie, you will tell me all about it."

He smiles as he lets the cat out of the bag.

He arranged this trip through Gerry, they are going to visit a space station on Pledas, one of the moons of the extrasolar gaseous planet, Ponmitz, which is four light years beyond our solar system. They will be travelling at a few times the speed of light, and will be there in two days. Gerry had only one condition, namely that they take a pilot. They will only need their space outfits when on Pledas.

"How long will we stay?"

"Two days. The station is a communication and exploration hub that maintains communication with passing travellors and it also sends travellors manned by humandroids to unknown areas to build up knowledge about them. We will stay in a two bedroom apartment and the staff there worked out a tour program for us in consultation with Bernie. We will basically be seeing what they are doing and learn about their results. Maybe they will also take us close to Ponmitz, if you want, naturally we cannot land there."

Melanie just smiles, "This sounds like the best holiday ever! You really outdid yourself this time, my husband, and I love you for it."

Bernie wakes them up early in the morning, with cheerful banter, "Approaching to land, Pablo and Melanie, I thought you would enjoy the scenery in the breaking light of day. Kindly don a space outfit as we will be alighting in one hour."

They both rush to the cockpit and join the pilot. With the darkness receding and the red of the sun sticking out its feelers, the view is breathtaking.

"Why are there so many lights . . . ?"

"They were built by the humandroid staff, as everything else in this world, naturally. It was felt they would make human visitors more comfortable, Pablo."

"And they were right—whoever they were, I feel at home already, don't you love?"

"For sure, Pabbie, anywhere with you is home—the past, the future, the stars, light years away . . ."

The rest of the descent is made in silence as they do not want to miss a thing.

After clearing a majestic mountain—the Hercules Mountains— they are now flying low as the land ahead is mostly flat and sandy, with more mountains in the distance. About a kilometre in front of them is a huge, colourful complex, the size of a small city, called Oasis. Oasis houses the human quarters, all serious maintainance work, the communications centre, the primary bases for all the humandroids and Pledas Control.

Their travellor turns to the east and heads straight for the dome, the passengers let out their whistling breaths when the dome opens to receive them and then closes behind them. They are in the transport hub, a huge area for receiving, sending off, parking, maintaining and servicing vehicles.

They hurry to put on their outfits—essentially a safety regulation—as the atmosphere in the dome is created for humans and was switched on and tested two days before they departed earth.

When the travellor's door opens, they are greeted by their welcoming party, Dean—the face of Pledas Control, and Rocco— their valet for the duration of the visit. They are taken to their living quarters on foot so that they can rest. Their apartment is in an area that resembles a typical middle class residential area from the 21st century! Each apartment stands alone, with a small yard and a garden in one corner.

At last they are inside, and after a quick walk through all the rooms, they curl up under the blankets.

"I feel like a king!"

"And I feel like a queen! I wonder . . . what is it like outside the dome?"

"Leave the crazy thoughts for Earth, my dear, goodnight. Or shall I say . . . good morning?"

He still waits for an answer when he hears her snoring softly and he falls asleep with a smile.

After visiting every inch of the city, talking to Rocco, Dean and a myriad other humandroids, the humans have completed a crash course on what occurs on Pledas, including the very geography of the moon and its parent planet. Now, as they are soaring back to Earth, Pablo wonders if it was just him or was the universe much smaller than in his time?

CHAPTER 15

———————◦•◦•◦•———————

Channel Century 20-21

T he entire family find themselves in the media room, watching Channel Century 20-21. The channel created separate sub-channels for various categories. Madeleine checks the list of sub-channels—history, science, culture, geography, animals, food, dances, lifestyle, health, medicine, sports, politics and music . . . The list goes on and on. She concentrates all her focus on the screen and calls for the ten most popular songs for the week in her head. The list opens in a small window.

"Mom! Dad! I did it! I did it!" She jumps up and down on the couch.

"Watch it; PA's going to scold you! You did what?"

"The mind thing, Dad. I controlled the TV with my mind!" She collapses on the couch, tired.

"Good going there, Maddie. I always said we girls are the brains of this family!"

"Come on, Brumin, we cannot leave things like this! Let's try to show them who's boss." Pablo gets into a bow-legged stance, points at the broadcast station and aims at it with one eye. "Is it working, Brumin? Is it working?"

"Sorry, Dad; try the other eye!"

The laughter reverberates through the house.

"Look at this list, Mom. They have a hit parade, but what is that number one—*Sylvia's Mother*—I don't know that . . ."

Melanie laughs. "I forgot about that song, it was popular for a while way back in the day, but it was really a classic; let's listen to it."

Actual footage of the band performing the song comes up. Though the song is not her type of music, Madeleine listens to it spellbound and has to bear with her father, who is singing along. She finds the passion and intensity with which the performance is delivered quite enjoyable. None of the music she really likes is on the hit parade.

"Number three is more up my alley . . . remember this one, Mel?" He breaks out into song, "Bye, bye, Miss American pie . . ." He keeps the note on the last word. "What I will do for some real pie now!"

Laughter reverberates through the house.

"They don't even have one hip-hop song on the list . . . Maybe they will still discover it," complains Brumin.

"God forbid! Thank heavens for that! Don't you agree, Mel?"

Melanie and Pablo laugh. After the song is finished, Brumin requests comments. Tens of thousands of people posted comments on the song, some even with tears in their eyes!

"Why are people so moved by this song?" Brumin sounds peevish.

Melanie engages channel control. "Control, we would like to know why people love this song so much; can you choose an item that will explain it?"

"Sure. There is a good analysis available by Anne Chatham coming up."

A young lady, dressed very casually in a shorts and jumper, appears on the screen. She has bright and lively eyes and her whole face tells a history of empathy, humility, love and laughter.

"I would like to share my love for a particular song with everyone. I discovered this amazing song while doing research; it is called *Sylvia's Mother*, performed by a band called *Dr. Hook and the Medicine Show*. The devotion with which it is performed grabbed me instantly. It strongly appeals to me as a woman, though I have no experience of the kind of reality it is about, but, of course, I have a lively imagination." Her eyes crinkle in the corners and almost close as she laughs heartily.

"The mother picks up the telephone to hear Sylvia's presumably ex-boyfriend asking to speak to her. The mother does not want to allow this connection and comes up with all sorts of excuses—she is busy, she is happy, and finally, she is on her way to be married! But the young man pleads and pleads; he will be brief, he pleads. He will only say goodbye, he tries. For some reason, the mother cannot simply put the phone down—she seems spellbound by this young man. In between the excuses, she throws in comments that subtly reveal the destructive nature of the relationship between the two young people and her desire to protect her child.

"The point is that, despite all her concerns for her beloved daughter, the mother ultimately gives in and asks him not to say anything that will spoil her daughter's plans. She also tells him which train Sylvia is going to take to get to her wedding!

"I think Sylvia and this young man are obviously passionately in love and should be together, but there is something destructive in both of them that every time ends in heartache for Sylvia and the two of them separating. I say both of them, though it appears the problem comes from the young man's side, but Sylvia keeps on going with him every time—therefore, she is also to blame.

"This going off and heartbreak is a cyclical occurrence because they just cannot stay away from each other for too long. Every time things fall apart, Sylvia is broken and moves back in with her mother. Poor angel mother adores her daughter soooo much and wants to protect her from this heartache and every time rebuilds Sylvia's life. Now, at last, her daughter can find happiness and protection in a marriage—but, just before she leaves for the wedding, lover boy phones again.

"Imagine the mother's anxiety! Is he going to wreck her daughter's life again? To protect her daughter, the mother must not let her speak to this young man, yet, in the end she gives in.

Why? Because the mother knows true love when she sees it. She knows her child is going to run to her lover and stay away for a while only to come back in pieces once more. But she is prepared to start all over again, because it is better to know heartache caused by true, genuine love than to be safe and protected in a marriage of convenience. So, the mother is herself complicit in this cycle of love and destruction! Beautiful, isn't it?" Her eyes crinkle again. "Now, that makes me think what kind of a life the mother must have had as a young woman; was it similar to Sylvia's or did she choose a marriage of comfort? That, I leave for someone else to explore. Bye."

By the time Anne has finished her analysis, she is smiling, but tears are rolling down her cheeks, and everybody else seems visibly moved too, everybody except Brumin, that is, who is gently rubbing his leg.

"Look at me, bawling like a baby," Pablo says as he flicks away a tear.

Madeleine and Melanie laugh as they do the same.

"It's a song, not a bloom'ng story," remarks the irascible Brumin, but they ignore him.

"I want to play it again," says Madeleine.

It seems as if they are listening to the song for the very first time; everyone listens attentively, including Brumin.

"Did you see number two on the list?" asks Madeleine afterwards.

"Yes . . . ." Melanie answers. "'*The Earth Song* by Michael Jackson; I don't know that song. Let's play it."

Even Brumin cannot help to sag into the back of his couch, letting the velvety admonishing voice warm the cockles of his heart.

Pablo wants to know what the most popular movie is, *Powder,* none of them knows it.

"Channel 20-21 Control," Brumin calls. "What is the ten most disliked features of Century 20-21? List them in order of priority, please."

A list opens in a small section of the screen:

1. Killings
2. Abuse of children
3. Failure to respect women
4. Money
5. Material inequality
6. Pornography
7. Racism
8. The disunity of the world
9. The conscious fomentation of ignorance by governments and the mainstream media
10. Widespread credulity

Melanie looks intently at the list; very interesting indeed, but this list requires some thinking. "Hey, guys, seeing this is about our time and our world, what do you think of this list?"

Brumin is stuck on the word 'credulity'. "Channel 20-21 Control, what is credulity?"

The reply flickers in the top left-hand corner. 'Credulity—disposition to believe something on little or no evidence'.

"Okay then, Mommy, it seems that the moderns do not like our society very much, but I do think we respected women . . . at least most of the time . . ."

"I don't think we should feel we need to defend our past," butts in Madeleine. "I see this list as the development of points of understanding and not as negative criticism . . ."

"This is also not scientific," remarks Pablo. "It's like the results of a poll and will probably change as more people submit their views."

"After all, modern society did develop out of the past societies, didn't it?"

"Yes, Daddy, it is the same humanity that is evolving. I so love it when my brain is stimulated . . . Let us look for more interesting things."

"Channel 20-21 Control, are any discussion papers published on the theme as yet?"

Pablo feels excitement starting to grip him too. A very long list of papers appears on the bottom right-hand side corner.

"Jeewizz! That's a long list; don't people sleep anymore?"

Pablo runs the remote control cursor from the top and his curiosity is quickly prickled . . .

"Jeewizz, Melanie, look at this one . . . 'How People in the 21st Century were Stumped by the Most Obvious Phenomena'. Control, bring me a digital copy, please."

A digital copy of the document separates from its source and moves right up to him in a small hologram screen. He uses his hand to position it in front of him and uses a finger to flip the pages. Digital reading, as this is called, is only recommended for short spells, paper and ink still favoured as the most friendly on human eyes.

"Look how cool this 3D document is, Mel. I'm even reading nowadays . . ."

"How you have changed over the years . . ." says Brumin wryly.

"Listen to this, Mel, then tell me what you think of it."

He reads from the introduction. "A fascicule. Fascicule, what the heck is that? Anyway, let's go on. From time immemorial, through the 21st century, humanity has been totally stumped by things all around them, things in front of their eyes and even inside them. This blindness has, in many cases, led to tremendous afflictions.

"Naturally, the list changed as scientific progress had been made; for instance, there was a time that people thought that the blue sky was a special place where heavenly beings resided! This continued throughout the 21st century.

"In this paper, I will lay emphasis on the three most obvious cases—to me—that still existed in the 21st century.

"Firstly, space. Unbelievably, despite amazing technological and intellectual progress, space was still seen as nothing, emptiness! It is common knowledge for millennia that there is no such thing as nothing. Nothing exists only as an intellectual construct; this much is common knowledge for millennia, but in this treatise I will try to elucidate the complex reasons why our peri-primitive ancestors felt the need to see in reality its opposite. Which need shared kinship with their desire to find the beginning (and the end) of the universe.

"The second major case is the fear of death. This leads straight back to our ancestors' conception of themselves. Death filled people with so much dread that they ended up not only spending huge amounts of time thinking and worrying about it, they created an entire imaginary existence in which they continued to live beyond their bodies and lives! In fact, the life after they died was regarded as being much, much better than the real one (provided they were good people)! Now one would think if they had this new life once they are dead, they would look forward to and be excited about entering that new life, but, quite the contrary, no; people then were extremely complicated. They did not wish to accept in all its ramifications the fundamental and obvious fact that we die because we live! That death is part of the privilege of life itself! People wanted to live, but not to die. It is like wanting to sit in the sun, but not wanting to get warm.

"Yes, life is nice, but all living things are at once an organism and matter, the former a form of the latter. Once life departs, the matter remains and undergoes transformation after transformation infinitely, and this—ironically—is the true afterlife!

"Today, we take for granted the matter-consciousness of life; in the epoch under discussion, such a concept would have been spurned. It took millennia before people could enjoy themselves as matter and see in themselves everything else and see everything else in them. See in themselves, like in everything else the finite and the infinite.

"Case number three is the blindness to the real meaning and worth of women. It was very difficult at first for me to believe that women were not appreciated and cherished as we do today, but quite the opposite, they were killed, raped, silenced, oppressed, enslaved, abused, hurt, insulted, bought, sold and further disrespected in numerous ways.

"I was very moved when I did this research. For the mothers of the world to have been treated so by people who were born into this world and suckled by women is, in my book, the most serious travesty of our past. Not only is the equality of men and women taken for granted today, we appreciate the fact that a man is only half a person if he does not find satisfaction in the love of a woman—so too the opposite.

"Moreover, it has been proven over and over that the single most beautiful thing in the entire universe is a woman. With all that we realise today about women, the way they have been treated during the 21st century is very hard to swallow. I do not know if society can ever make up for this heinous history, but, for my part, I dedicate this paper to all the women of the world. I beg the reader's forgiveness for entering into such a lengthy introduction, but I just could not stop myself . . ."

"Now that is quite something, Pablo. That is really deep. I don't know about you, but I am still afraid of death; I certainly hope to go to Heaven . . . Maybe we are already there? I am certainly going to read that paper and think about everything . . ."

"I certainly like what he wrote about women. Can you print it, Daddy?" Madeleine wants to know.

"Amazing stuff, bloody amazing . . . Yes, definitely, Maddie; I want to read the whole thing tonight. Estienne, how do I get this printed?"

"I am sending it to your bedroom printer, but let me show you how to do it manually . . ." He presses on the hologram.

"Look at this one . . . Control, bring me a digital copy, please." Madeleine's voice is a mixture of confusion and interest. She starts to read,

"Many people, even adults, were afraid of what were called ghosts! Dear reader, you may wonder what a ghost was, well it was something like a living spiritual essence of someone who was dead. Ghosts had the ability to Interact with people and to even hurt them. I find it so fascinating that adults could be afraid of something that did not really exist. Today, even small children would find the very concept of ghosts funny!"

She looks up, "Is anyone here still afraid of ghosts? I think I'm over that. What do you say Brumin?"

"Well, when I was dead I did not become a ghost . . . so, no, I no longer think they exist." The parents also deny believing in ghosts any longer. Both admit to believing in ghosts before, though.

That night, Pablo cannot sleep; he reads and reads, stops for a while, thinks and thinks, then, later, he starts making brief notes for further reflection and he goes on like this until the sun finds him sitting in his study.

Can you guess what the most popular novel is? Why, at a ninety-five percent approval rating, none other than Rudyard Kipling's *The Jungle Book*! Movies of the book were dug up, but discarded in dismay for not doing justice to such a great work. Scores of new movies were made, in which the language and childlikeness of the animals were brought out to reflect the original masterpiece as closely as possible.

People talk about the book everywhere they go. Children and adults alike can be heard mimicking the style of the dialogue. It is not uncommon to hear recitals of lines from the book, such as, 'ye chooses and ye chooses not. What is this talk of choosing?' and much more. But favourite are the various songs in the book. At any time, you can hear sky-hoppers reciting the most popular *Night-song in the jungle*,

'Now Chil the Kite brings back the night
 that Mang the Bat sets free.
 Herds are shut in byre and hut
 for loosed till dawn are we.
 This is the hour of pride and power,
 of talon and tush and claw . . .' and on and on they would go.

The whole society is similarly hypnotised by *Sylvia's Mother*, which has spawned an entire industry of its own. The footage of the song is displayed in house art across the globe. Musical groups make their own renditions of the song. Dramas are staged and television productions are made. Poems and novellas are written. Artists bring forth renditions and impersonations of all kinds, and babies worldwide are named Sylvia—even a few boys!

Despite all the horrors, violence, ignorance and pornography that is uncovered—and unceremoniously discarded—many, many gems of the 20th and 21st centuries are brought into the light of day. These gems shine some brilliant light into the misty tunnel that was Century 20-21.

And you better believe it, society has unearthed bountiful and splendid cultural treasures, but they cannot cover the shame of much that is raised from the dead.

CHAPTER 16

——— •::◄○⊃○○⊂►::• ———

House of Primitive Human Brutality

I t is late afternoon and the sun will be setting soon. There are only a few clouds in the blue sky and the breeze is lazy and as light as it can be while still qualifying as wind. The Adam family are amongst the specially selected guests who come from all corners of the Earth to attend the opening of the House of Primitive Human Brutality. Madeleine, her parents and brother are totally aghast. They are sitting on the lawn of one of the most famous buildings of their time! It is huge—must be built true to size. Between them and the monument is a raised platform on which the officials are seated, with four empty seats between them.

The journey, in a travellor, was short and their pilot, Chantushka, was very engaging and pleasant.

Nadhezda opens the proceedings.

"Ladies and gentlemen," she says in a pleasant, orotund voice, "I greet you in the name of the Council of the Realm and I thank you for taking the effort to be in attendance. I would like the Adam family to please come up here and take these seats provided for them." She smiles at them and waves to the vacant seats.

Their movement to the stage is greeted with loud applause.

"It is really such a coincidence that this monument in front of you (and behind me) hails from their time.

"To Pablo, Melanie, Madeleine and Brumin, let me take this opportunity to extend a very special welcome to you. And I speak for all of humanity when saying that you are all helping us such a lot by just being here. The crisis that this monument is trying to help address has causes that are very deep and that stretch beyond the discovery of the time capsule way, way back into time and into the labyrinths of the ever-evolving human mind. Dealing with this can only make us stronger as a species and I once again thank the Adam family for joining us tonight.

"Now, I am not a member of the committee—just a pundit—so I call on the Committee of the House of Primitive Human Brutality to explain and contextualise the monument for us. Let us hear a loud applause for Valdoran . . ." He stands up and bows. ". . . Laurie . . ." She does the same. ". . . And Chrizelle." She does the same. "Over to you guys."

Chrizelle moves to the front.

"On behalf of the committee, I welcome everyone present and also all the viewers who are sharing this event with us. We prepared a brief presentation for today and also a lengthy interactive one for deeper study. But, before we begin, I have something important to say. Although the choice of monument comes from the time of the Adam family, it obviously has nothing at all to do with them. We sincerely hope that our special guests will not feel any blame or guilt for what will be presented here today, because they are rather victims; in other words, this monument is also established in their honour. Control, we are ready to begin."

Suddenly, the platform starts to slowly move to the side of the gathering. Where it was five minutes before, the area turns into a visual hologram extravaganza. What was enacted on this lawn brought forth a river of tears from four billion eyes.

The hologram presentation was in the form of a narration with life-sized moving images for illustration. The hour was scarcely enough for people to internalise the images of genocides, massacres, wars, nuclear explosions, executions, assassinations, slavery and criminal murders. The presentation laid special emphasis on one country that killed more people than any other country in all of history.

Afterwards, Brumin turned to his dad next to him. "I never thought of it in this way, Dad, so, beneath all that glamour and power they liked to display, all this blood and barbarism were lurking."

"Exactly what I am thinking, Brumin."

Brumin smirks. "They certainly killed a lot of people, more than a hundred million, it seems; how did they sleep at night?"

After the presentation, the stage moves to its original place while everybody is catching their breath and regaining their composure; the Adams wipe tears of shame. Valdoran gives a verbal elucidation.

"A question may be raised as to why we single out one country when the problem we are dealing with was universal, but this country bears the largest responsibility for the deaths of innocents in all history. We chose this building as the monument, because it is the most famous symbol associated with this country.

"Firstly, the nation whose political centre this was, was a nation of invaders who founded their country on the extermination of the original inhabitants. Tens of millions of men, women and children—robbed of their lives in the biggest genocide ever. These invaders massacred with their guns people who were armed only with sharpened sticks. We salute these victims, the bravest of the bravest, and we remember them.

"Then there were the tens of millions of people who lost their lives as a result of the slave trade, who died either during the journey, were killed by their owners or who died premature deaths as a result of the savagery they were exposed to. We salute each of these victims and we remember them.

"There were the millions of people who were blown up with nuclear bombs by the leaders of this nation, including those who died after the events from all sorts of radiation illnesses for hundreds of years. We salute each and every one of these victims and we remember them.

"We remember the millions who were killed in countries too many to list. We remember all the civilians killed in the many wars unleashed by this country. Not to be forgotten are the total support given by these leaders to innumerable wars and assassinations by their friends around the world.

"There were the millions of deaths that these leaders were responsible for during the age of revolutions during the twenty-first century that threw out the old order and ushered in the new.

"As if all of this was not enough, these leaders of death used horrific cluster bombs and ammunition contaminated with depleted uranium in many of their unjust wars in poorer countries, which led to the rapid increase of birth defects in those countries. Drone assassinations had become a daily dose of death.

"There were the deaths of millions of people in China and Russia as a result of the final wars caused by these leaders, who, in the end, had become totally out of their minds as they tried to prevent their tottering empire from collapsing. There were the millions of people who died as a result of secretive activities of death initiated by the barbaric leaders of this nation across the globe.

"We honour and remember each and every one of these victims as well as all the other victims of human brutality. Now, let us look again at the monument . . ."

In the blink of an eye, the monument turns blood red with the appearance of blood dripping from the sky onto the top of the building!

"Once a day, for ten minutes, the colour will switch. Red is to remind us of the life blood of all the victims that this monument is honouring—and just maybe it will help us all to wash away the stain of this history of lament."

After the presentation, the entourage goes into the building, visiting every room. Each room or space is dedicated to one of the various atrocities in the most elaborate sense imaginable.

The reception hall, especially, blows everybody away; the Adams remain in it the longest. It has a poster dedicated to each leader, highlighting on a map the places where his or her decisions had caused innocent human beings to be killed. An overlay of all the maps is done on a digital poster with a shocking result.

Brumin cannot help it, but he feels deeply ashamed and partly responsible for what he has seen—even though he did not even live in most of those times mentioned or in the country concerned. He remembers the last leader of this country that he knew, a nice, humane guy at first; he really thought the election in that country of their first alternative president would change things around, but it clearly did not; things seem to have worsened from then. He remembers never liking history at school. Never did he realise just how real it all was. Yet, he feels awed at being inside this building, a little at home in this place . . .

PART THREE

THE DEVIL HIDES IN THE DETAILS

CHAPTER 17

Dark Stirrings

Since the problems with Melanie's adaptation surfaced, the Council of the Realm and Adam Family Control increased their efforts to ensure that all the family members are coping satisfactorily with their new lives. The sessions between the doctor-scientists and their patients have been increased to weekly appointments.

Egbert, Brumin's doctor-scientist, has been visiting him likewise to find out how he has been doing. During his visits, Egbert would always come back to Brumin's memories of his death, but every time he feels as if he comes up against a brick wall. Time after time, he comes up with a new angle in an attempt to explore his patient's emotions with respect to that night. Brumin always tells him that he remembers what happened and how it happened, but that the memories elicit no emotion from him. It seems like something that happened in a dream. He is not worried about it—only happy to be alive again.

Though the doctor-scientist never before worked with anyone who did not speak freely of what he or she felt, he picked up that Brumin was not entirely forthcoming. He spent hours upon hours thinking about his patient, trying to figure out if he missed any signs—but he came up with nothing. He thought a lot about the way Brumin would just stare vacantly ahead of him—just stare, or absent-mindedly rub just above his right knee or give economical answers, as short as possible. He discussed this with Adam Family Control, who told him that the best course of action is for him to continue his sessions with Brumin and to file a monthly report with it.

What he does not tell Egbert, what he does not tell anybody, is that he is really haunted by that night. After two weeks, he started waking up in the middle of the night with the fear of death in him, clutching his right leg where he was shot. Then he would struggle to fall asleep. Soon, he started to dread going to sleep.

From deep in his bosom, a disturbing feeling started to build up slowly, as if in concentric circles. Circles of anguish and anger. At first, he could not understand it, until that one night when he woke up again, clutching his leg, drenched in sweat, face contorted with fright, and a word slipped to the fore in his head like a pip squeezed from an overripe fruit—*revenge!*

From then on, a new feeling took hold of him and it grew. This emotion made him feel relaxed in an icy sort of way, but soon it developed an urgent edge. It started to push him; something had to give; something had to break.

This escalating yearning for vengeance combined a little later with the nasty side of the old Brumin that no one knew of but him.

Brumin. Mommy's boy who could never do anything wrong. Brumin. Mommy's boy who was spoilt into the ground. At the time he died, he was a very troubled young man—very troubled indeed. The day he got out of his regeneration casket, he felt as fresh as a daisy, no sign of the deep, dark sombreness that had shrouded his mind before and nudged him down that bottomless pit of darkness. Then, suddenly, just like that, it was back. He was like a lone boatman without oar or rudder in a tempest, riding out a huge wave fed by two rivers of woeful feelings. He never was strong on will power, for, whenever circumstances tested him and he had the opportunity to grow stronger through solving one of life's problems, Mommy would step in.

This is a night like so many others, but this time there is a difference.

Brumin wakes up drenched in cold sweat. He checks the hologram clock on the wall: 2:30. As if a strange force has got hold of him—he has to get up, get out. Within his anxiety, he feels the comfort of familiarity—déjà vu!

He dresses slowly, like a zombie, then goes to the kitchen and looks in the cutlery drawer. He finds a knife and runs one finger over the blade. *Ah . . . very sharp.* As he leaves, he makes sure no eyes—human or otherwise—see him slip out. All their PAs are retired for the evening, but can self-reactivate within seconds. Outside, he looks to see if no one else is about. Like a thief in the night, he slinks from one tree to the next, staying in the shadows, this time not admiring the graffiti—as he calls the wall art. Not knowing where he is going—always covered by a tree or dwelling. After slinking around like this for about half an hour, he sees a cute pet tiger urinating in a garden and the compelling urge that seizes him is unstoppable.

He approaches the pet with a smile on his face, sits next to it, rubbing its cheeks, then, without warning, still smiling, he slits the animal's throat. After his grisly deed, he wipes the knife on the grass, throws sand over the bloody evidence and takes off, holding the warm corpse by one leg. Staying in the shadows, he makes his way to the thick forest on the outskirts of the suburb and hurls his prey among the trees. Memories flood back of how he killed that dog many years ago . . . Ah, it feels good.

Then he takes off again. Faster and faster, he runs. He feels relieved. But the more he runs, the more frustrated he becomes, because he cannot run away from whatever is chasing him.

The forest is far behind him; he is now running on the lawn of the House of Primitive Human Brutality. He grabs an old-fashioned lamp post with one hand and runs around it. Faster and faster, he swings. Faster, faster, faster! Around and around he goes, feeling utterly delirious. Faster and faster and faster till his hand slips free and he swirls around and around, arms outstretched, until he collapses with his back on the dewy grass.

His chest heaves violently with anxiety and excitement. This feels good, liberating. He laughs. But he knows he cannot do it again. As his body cools down in the evening air under the accusing eye of the frowning moon, he turns on his side, looks at the monument and shudders. Captivated by the majesty of the complex, he finds that he cannot look away—it is beckoning him. As he manages to tear his eyes away, he hatches an elaborate plot, as if with its help. He walks home slowly, calmly chewing over his plan.

He gets up after only three hours of sleep, feeling refreshed.

"Good morning, Brumin."

"Good morning, PM. I had a short, but great, sleep, thank you."

"I am concerned about the disruptions in your sleep, Brumin, as well as the level of anxiety I detected. It emanates from every cell in your body. I could only treat the symptoms with aromatherapy. I recommend much more sleep, regular exercise and at least two hours a day of reading for relaxation."

"Okay, PM . . . I will think about it, thanks, but you worry too much. I am okay."

That day, Brumin is as happy as a lark. He makes jokes with everyone in the house—even the PAs—listens to loud music and sings along just as loudly. His mother knows she should be happy, but she is not and she doesn't know why.

CHAPTER 18

Useful Citizens

Breakfast at the Adams. Brumin finds his family enjoying breakfast around the kitchen table, watching the morning broadcasts.

"Look there, Brumin, a pet animal disappeared two nights ago—can you imagine this is world news? The family is quite cut up about it and tens of thousands of people have already sent messages of sympathy!"

"Amazing people, Dad. What are they going to do about it?"

"Searching for the pet has been worked into the daily service rota. I hope they find the critter alive and well." He raises his voice slightly. "Listen, guys, we have had enough of a holiday. I am sure we all decided by now how we will spend our thirty hours of meaningful activity per week? We must not let these kind people wait for us unnecessarily. Come, let us tell our PAs; you first, Brumin?" He calls all the PAs.

Melanie backs him up, "Yeah, guys, Dad is right; we have been hemming and hawing over this for too long and these kind people have just been too patient with us . . ."

Madeleine says, "Dad, Mom, I would like to have a pet . . . An elephant. Would you mind . . . ?"

"I would mind," answers Brumin. "Protocol ZeeZee20 Pee declares that people must clean up after their own pets and Maddie has forgotten how to work . . ."

She throws him with a small coaster. "You forgot how to work seven thousand years ago! I must admit, I do not know how to use the cleaning appliances, but PA can show me; right, Sipho?"

"Of course, Madeleine."

"I don't see a problem, Maddie. I also want a pet; I'll take a . . . a . . . ummmm . . . Siberian tiger. PA, can you request these pets for us?"

"As long as it does not bite my elephant!"

They laugh.

"Yes, Melanie, I will also arrange for their shelters, food deliveries and medical visitations."

"And a wolf for me, please, and a gorilla for Dad!"

They laugh.

"One gorilla in the house is enough, Sipho," adds Melanie

"Fine, Brumin."

The family banter continues until Pablo clears his throat loudly. "Now back to the business at hand." He sounds a little impatient. "PA, I want to work in two places—the laboratory where we were regenerated and in the monument. This will help me come to terms with my own history as well as my new life. Also, I want to follow a course of study on regeneration."

Madeleine says, "I would like to study astronomy and work in an observatory or any similar place."

Pablo says, "I want to work anywhere I am allocated so that I can learn a variety of things. I would like to study weapons; is that possible?"

Melanie says, "Can I teach, PA?"

"Unfortunately not. Children are taught by their parents until the age of four. Thereafter, their teachers are humandroids."

"Okay, then I want to be part of the Bloodless Oceans Project and I will study whatever I can to cope with the project."

The PAs forwarded the requests to Adam Family Control. Affirmative replies are relayed almost immediately.

"Brumin, I am told there is no one working at the House of Primitive Human Brutality. The tours are fully automated. Adam Family Control will create a service station for you in there from where you will oversee all activities concerning the monument. I will report back at breakfast tomorrow."

"Thanks, PA . . . that's so cool."

Everyone mistakes the thin smile flashing across his teeth.

Humandroids can be used to perform all functions required by humans, but such a possibility is frowned upon as decadent, uncultured and un-human. All adults spend thirty-five meaningful hours per week on service and study. No one is forced to, but this is a social expectation.

Adults decide on their course of study, but they are moved from service station to service station. The focus is on service, exposure and learning. The Adam family just looked at each other when a PA once explained to them that, to their society, the category of human in the past who deserves the least respect after murderers, other serious criminals and exploiters of the vulnerable constitutes those who spent their lives in perpetual leisure. One ten-year-old had apparently written an award-winning essay on them in which she called them 'empty money-heads'. It was the first time they heard a humandroid laugh.

Work, or service, as it is called, is both a human necessity and a joy. The Adams are to decide what service they want to perform and for how long. They may change their choice at their convenience.

Madeleine wanted to know more about the Bloodless Oceans Project, so her PA was delighted to explain it.

After society succeeded in eliminating the shedding of human blood, it was decided—over three thousand years ago—to work towards removing bloodletting from nature, in as far as is practical. As part of this project, all large carnivores and omnivores on land (excluding humans) were genetically altered so that they are now vegetarian and many have been reduced in size. After this was achieved, the focus moved to the oceans. It is estimated that this phase of the plan will take another thousand years.

"But . . . But is this not messing with nature? I remember that our society went all out to protect the natural way of things."

"Messing with nature, Madeleine?" asked Sipho. "Certainly not. We are improving nature according to human values. Do not forget that humans are part of nature. It is believed today that humans are the highest known form of the evolution of nature. The brain of humans is, in fact, the brain of the universe. In other words, through the evolution of humans, nature developed its own brain. The human brain, even in your time as you just now mentioned, Madeleine, concerned itself not only with social matters, but with nature itself. Great deeds such as protecting the environment and travelling to other heavenly bodies for research purposes were the predecessors of the grand projects of the current epoch. The role of humans is to improve nature."

Brumin wants to know more about weaponry and military defence, and Boris is only too eager to explain.

As the world lives in total unity and harmony, premeditated threats to the world's safety are seen—hypothetically—as emanating from beyond our solar system. However, this is total conjecture at the moment because no sign of non-microscopic life beyond Earth has been detected. Still, the world is armed to the teeth to confront any such threat, and the weaponry is developed continually.

Every year, the people working in the weaponry and defence sector form three teams. Two teams prepare to defend Earth against an imaginary scenario that is developed by Council Control based on views canvassed from the broader population. So far, all scenarios have been of alien invasions with the differences being the technological level and weaponry of the invaders, as well as the point at which the invasion is detected. The first team are the invaders and they develop an invasion programme for Cyber War Games. Their weapons are not based on science and their imaginations have only the sky as the limit. The other two teams separately develop real weapons and tactics in secret. They then load their defence programmes on Cyber War Games, but they can only include existing weapons or their own inventions that have been successfully tested.

At the beginning of December, the 'war' begins. Each team gets a chance to defend the Earth and is given points for its defence. The war is watched by all on their media screens and is judged by Council Control. The team (or both teams) that manages to defeat the invaders wins the Saviours of the World trophy or trophies. In the event of both defending teams being successful, the one that scores the higher points receives Heroes of the World medals.

If the invaders beat both teams, they receive the Masters of the Earth trophy. All winning teams defend their titles the following year.

At the end of the competition, the Military Committee, which consists only of humandroids, studies all the weapons used and produces en masse weapons they think will advance the Earth's defence capabilities. They also use the opportunity to review all existing defence equipment and policies and make changes where they deem necessary. All soldiers are specially produced humandroids that are stored for the day they may be required.

As this explanation progresses, Brumin's eyes glitter with excitement and he is on the verge of changing his choices when a dark shadow suddenly douses the flame and he sags back in his chair.

"Are you all right, son?"

"Yes, Dad. I am just tired . . . enjoy yourself with the computer games." He yawns lazily.

CHAPTER 19

⬥ ═══◆◦○◦◆═══ ⬥

Brumin's Barbecue

2:30. Brumin's eyes open as if they were programmed. He readies himself and slinks out of the house for his nocturnal activity, bag in hand with a long knife in it.

He finds himself in the forest, venturing deeper than before. He walks slowly, looks around; many pathways, medium-sized trees, very tall trees. He sees animals sleeping between the trees, sets his sights on a small deer sleeping on its own.

He walks right up to it, as all these animals are totally unafraid of anything, not having had any enemies for thousands of years. He puts his arm around its neck and stabs his knife deep into its chest. The animal is too shocked to make a sound and limply falls to the ground, looking deep into Brumin's eyes before closing its own for the last time. Brumin stabs the dead animal in a frenzy until he is exhausted; the animals nearby just moan and run away into the night.

After resting a short while, he sets to work. Makes a fire and, while it burns, he cuts off a hind leg, then he separates it at the knee and pulls as much of the skin off the thigh as he can. When the coals are ready, he positions the thigh over them on a contraption he made with sticks. He turns the meat every now and then, and the fat starts to slowly drip onto the coals, making a sizzling sound as it burns. *Ahhhhhh.* He breathes in that wonderful smell he had been missing so much; it brings back the fondest memories.

He sits and looks into the fire, the smell of burning animal fat and tissue momentarily blanking his mind.

At last, the meat is ready; he devours his hefty portion with relish and licks his fingers for an eternity, then a silly feeling suddenly grabs hold of him. He cools a dash of ash and smears lines across his cheeks and forehead. Then, knife held high in one hand and the thigh bone in the other, he performs a bow-legged warlike dance around the dying fire, hooting like an owl.

A chirping bird brings him back to reality and he quickly hides the dead animal under some brushes and throws soil over the coals before taking the trail back home.

On the way back, he savours the first meat he has eaten for millennia—albeit clandestinely—but he realises it was not really the meat he had hungered for. It was the kill he enjoyed and devouring what he had killed.

In the ensuing months, Brumin repeats this night-time activity a few times, turning the forest into his personal hunting ground. Then he replaces his hunting sessions with another, more grotesque programme.

CHAPTER 20

────── ◦═╣◦◖✦◗◦╠═◦ ──────

Madeleine's Awe

P ablo is resting in the lounge after his first day of work when Madeleine looks for him, more bright-eyed and bushy-tailed than always.

"Hullo, Dad. How was your first day as an active member of society?"

"Quite terrific, sweetie; I am still overwhelmed by what I saw—they put me in the catering department. It is huuuge—amazing really—how was your first day?"

"Dad, I found out some stuff that I don't know if people knew in our time. For instance, space that we used to take for granted as empty nothingness is actually the most important physical part of the universe!"

"Remember I read a paper that mentioned it, but I did not quite understand it, Maddie, but this sounds interesting. Go on."

"In our time, Dad, we did not realise that space and matter are inescapably connected. In fact, space is a form of matter, or, rather, matter is a form of space!"

He laughs at the amazement in her voice and on her face. "So, what comes first, the egg or the chicken or the chicken feed?"

"Dad, you are joking, but you actually hit the nail on the head . . ."

"Woa . . . Slow down there! . . . how so?"

"There is no *before*; I mean, in the universe, everything was always there, only changing from one form into another. There was always matter as we know it, and also space, which is now called primo. Space, or primo, is not nothing, Dad; it's a kind of supra-matter that actually produces matter all the time. Primo does not consist of atoms, but it is rather like a continuous thin soup that constantly forms primal-particles that develop into a pre-atomic plasma, which gives birth to atoms. The particles and plasma are forms of pre-matter and, once the atoms are formed, we have matter as we know it. Matter can also not exist outside primo, which not only surrounds it, but is a part of all atoms. Atoms form an atomic ether, which, under the forces of latent energy, electromagnetism, quantity, attraction and pressure transforms into atomic plasma, which develops into a kind of energy gas, which, in the next stage of its evolution, explodes and results in the heavenly bodies we have . . ."

"Okay, okay, let me see . . . so, who made the primo?"

"Daaad. Like matter, primo is infinite and timeless! No one made it, but whereas primo has no form, matter changes from one form to another ad infinitum, but each of its forms has a beginning and an end."

"My baby sounds so clever; what is ad infinitum?"

"On and on forever, Dad."

Pablo, being a practical man, lost her a long time ago, but he enjoys her excited rambling. "Oh, and what about the big bang?"

"No big bang, Dad, but all sorts of bangs have been and still are taking place all the time!"

"Gee, Maddie, I have to go lie down now, I have a headache."

"Wait, wait, Dad. Most of our scientists were looking in the wrong places. They were looking for the start to the universe. But the universe has no beginning and no end. They never saw all-important space as part and actual mother of the universe. Because humans deal with matter all the time, we are aware that it has a beginning and an end, meaning that it ages. However, if we change our mindset to realise that matter ages within the framework of a non-aging primo, things begin to look different."

"So what are you saying about how everything started?"

"The birth of matter cannot be traced back to its origin, because we cannot go to the start of the infinite. People are now no longer obsessed with the origins of the universe. Isn't this beautiful stuff, Dad?"

He laughs. "Monstrous! I understood one percent of what you said, but even that little is quite mind-boggling. You must tell me more next time."

"Wait, Dad, let me tell you about time."

He sits down again. "Okay, sweetie, I am all ears."

"Time is a condition of matter as we know it and exists only as far as matter is concerned. As I said, primo is time-free. Time measures the chronological development of all forms of matter from its birth. What causes the aging of matter is called the Chronos Boson, which is a name for the particle hidden inside the nucleus of all atoms, which had eluded scientists for thousands of years. This particle emits a steady force that ages its atom at a rate that is uneven across the universe. Primo does not have a Chronos Boson."

"All I can say is, wow, my girl, you learnt such a lot in one day and you used to suck at science! You even sound different, so intelligent. I need a drink to settle my nerves, but I picked up one thing in all you said. Primo is actually the perfect one. Matter seems to be a sort of degeneration of primo that is why it is always destroyed in the end."

"Dad, you got it! But do not say destroyed because matter cannot be destroyed."

"Right! Right! I got it . . . I think! Why does matter alone have this Chrono Boso thing?"

"Chronos Boson, Dad, Chronos Boson. It is because the Chronos Boson is formed out of parts of the different particles that make up an atom. So any pre-atom phenomena can automatically not have one!"

He leaves the room laughing and quite impressed with his little girl, who is not less impressed with him. Still on a high, Maddie goes to her study to do some more research on this exciting field she has discovered.

What she did not tell her father is that she met this amazing young man at her workplace, the Centre for Astronomical Research. He was busy conducting an experiment when her tutor introduced her to him. Serge is his name. Serge . . . What a beautiful name! When he turned to look at her, she could see how nervous he was. She hopes he did not see how stunned she looked when their eyes met. Her melting heart gave a leap in her chest and it felt as if he could see inside her. Luckily, they turned away to continue with their tour, just in time so that she could hide the redness flushing her face. She is just happy he did not say anything to her, for she would not have been able to reply, with her throat all choked up.

Talking to her dad helped her get him out of her mind for a while. She wonders if she will ever see him again. Her wrist communicator buzzes, indicating an incoming message. She checks the message. *Oh my God, it is Serge!* Below a tiny photo of him is the message; Serge would like to speak to Madeleine, touch if accepted. She jumps up! What does he want? In her consternation, she runs to her room and gets under the blanket! *What am I going to say?* She rips off her wrist communicator and throws it onto the bedside pedestal.

She takes a deep breath and starts to talk to herself. "Come on, Maddie; stop being silly."

She puts it back on her wrist and goes to the media room.

She uses her mind to call him. He appears on the screen—and she on his. He looks very nervous; this makes her feel a bit more in control.

"Hello, Madeleine—how are you?"

"I am fine, thank you. How are you?"

Both choose their words very carefully.

"I am fine. Have you been sky-hopping yet?"

"No, I do not know how, but it looks very exciting."

"I would like to show you how; can I pick you up in one hour? I will bring equipment for you."

"Okay, but make it two hours. See you then. Bye."

"Bye for now, Madeleine."

Water, she needs water to cool down. She must regain her composure before he arrives. She must look her best. *Oh my God, I think he likes me!* She runs off with her heart throbbing in her ears.

It doesn't seem like two hours when her PA sends a message to her wrist-communicator that her visitor is waiting for her in the living room. She checks the time . . . *Hmm he is right on time.* Her PA mentioned to her that promptitude is held in high esteem. She collects him.

"Hi, Serge! I'm ready, shall we go?"

"Is it possible to meet your parents?"

This threw her off-guard; she did not even tell them she was going out. They come after she calls them.

"Mom, Dad, this is Serge; we met at work. He is going to show me how to sky-hop."

After the introductions, they leave. She is surprised to see that he came with a travellor. They hop in,

"This is Pat. Pat, this is Madeleine."

"Pleased to meet you, Madeleine; as you can see, I am your pilot for the evening."

"Nice meeting you, Pat."

"I am not allowed to pilot until I am twenty years of age. I don't mind, as I enjoy being ferried around."

"Only two more months, Serge," says Pat reassuringly.

"Is it easy for young people to get a travellor with a pilot if they want to go somewhere?"

"Nothing is easier, you merely call—or ask your PA to call—Transportation Services."

"You know, Serge, in my day, things were not so easy. Most people struggled very hard to get the things they needed and most never got what they needed."

"I can hardly imagine that. I have been doing some research on your era; I would like to discuss some of the things I discovered, some time. Do you want to know where we are going?"

"Yes."

"Pat is going to drop us at the nearest park."

Suddenly, another travellor comes right at them and they jerk to the side as it appears to bounce away.

"What just happened?" She cannot hide the fear in her voice as she is still clutching her armrest.

Serge briefly puts his hand reassuringly on her shoulder. "Vehicles cannot collide ever, or hit a living being or humandroid. They are made like that. Are you okay?"

"Yes, sorry."

Just then, the face of a flustered young man appears on the central screen. "Hello, I'm Cal. I'm so sorry that I scared you; I was just kissing my beloved for one moment—or for what seemed like one moment, and whoops. Sorry again, gotta go."

Serge answers, "Not to worry, Cal. No harm done . . . take care and say hi to your sweetheart. Bye."

In the park, Serge helps her put on the levitation boots and the control wristband.

"The boots are made of specially processed noble metals, giving it gravity defying qualities that are controlled by pushing this switch to the left to levitate and to the right to land." He points to her wristband.

"The highest you will be able to go is roughly roof height. Are you good at keeping your balance?" He smiles broadly, looking directly into her eyes.

"No ways." She gives a nervous smile.

"Hold onto me until you get the hang of it."

He hooks his right arm into her left. She gets a nice cosy, warm feeling.

"Now we both push our switches slowly to the left."

Her legs turn to jelly as they both rise slowly; had he not been holding her arm, she would probably have somersaulted endlessly!

"We move by using mainly our legs, but we have to use our entire bodies! You have to sort of surge, like this." He lifts his right leg, bends it by the knee and pushes forward hard.

She follows his lead. It doesn't feel like she is walking on air; it is more like space-walking, but with a little control! After about thirty minutes, she can keep her balance while moving. Once she has won her independence and confidence, she hops away from him. "Come on, Serge! Let's see who is first on top of that tree!"

He is past her in a flash. They play around like that for over an hour. Serge shows her all sorts of sky-hopping tricks. They dash here and there until they practically collapse in the park with exhaustion. After they panted for a few minutes, Serge points out some of the star constellations and planets. So they lie and chat without realising the passage of time, until Pat brings the travellor over.

Serge sits up, startled, "It's getting late; we had better get back before your parents come looking for us!"

Serge sees her off at her front door. "I had a most wonderful time, Madeleine; can I visit you again tomorrow night?"

Her smile dazzles him. "Yes, Serge, let's do something together tomorrow. Have a good night."

She has hardly closed the door when she texts her mom a message.

'Mom, I have something to tell you; get me in the kitchen for a glass of ambrosia'.

Melanie wakes up when her wrist communicator beeps on the pedestal. Yawning, she reads the message and gets up lazily.

As she walks into the kitchen, Madeleine pushes the button on the wall bar, requesting two cups of warm ambrosia. While she waits for her yawning mother to fully wake up, she admires the elegant and fully automated beverage bar with its display screen and buttons. There are over a hundred beverages that can be requested and received within seconds in cups that are continuously recycled by placing them back in the machine after rinsing them.

"When I am with him, I feel happy and silly at the same time. I am afraid he won't like me enough. I want to look my best and be my best when I am with him. I feel like I am in a dream and my heart feels so warm and comfortable when I am with him. Is this love? It must be . . ."

Melanie interrupts the torrent of words, "Wait a minute, Maddie, hold your horses now. Breathe, girl, breathe!"

She laughs.

"Of course you are in love. Where did you two go?"

Mother and daughter talk into the wee hours of the morning. Melanie feels such warmth around her heart; since Maddie was sixteen years old, they stopped having heart to hearts. She doesn't know what went wrong, but is only too happy that things between them have changed for the better.

CHAPTER 21

—✦✦◈◆◈✦✦—

Madeleine's Love

During the next three weeks, Serge and Madeleine spend a lot of time together. They go sky-hopping, visit Serge's friends, go to sports matches, to the theatre, visit the forest, take trips together overseas and into space, go on nature walks, and just are together.

On a visit to their favourite park one evening, Serge spreads a picnic blanket, pulls her down next to him, holds both her hands and declares his undying love for her.

"Madeleine, I love you. I loved you from the first moment I saw you. Since our eyes met that first day, I have been walking on air without my sky-hoppers; my heart is filled with joy and warmth at the thought of you. You are my first thought when I wake up and my last before I fall asleep. I burn to hold you and cherish you in my arms. Will you be my beloved? I promise to hold you dearest in my heart forever."

She expected something like this even a while ago already, but not like this. She almost faints. She pulls herself together, kisses him gently on his lips, pulls her head back and gives him a smile like he has never seen before.

"For ever and ever . . . me your beloved, you my beloved, but, if you want another kiss, you must catch me first!"

She jumps up and dashes away, laughing, but he has his arms around her in two minutes. He holds her tight. "Thank you, my love, thank you! Now for my reward . . ."

They end up lying on their backs next to each other, like so many times before, only this time they lie hand in hand. They look at the stars in silence. Madeleine puts her head on his chest and he strokes her forehead. She looks at the stars and smiles.

"Look, Serge, the stars are smiling at us."

He points to the sky. "That one is saying something to me . . ."

"Oh, and what is it saying?"

"That I must kiss you for him."

"Oh, it's a boy star."

They both laugh as they roll in each other's embrace.

"Maddie . . ."

"Yes?"

She strokes his hand.

"My service will come to an end in one week. I will then move on. I do not even know where Service Control will place me. I will miss seeing you at work, but I will see you at every opportunity. I just love you so much and I just want to be with you, but I suppose I have to control myself."

"Aww, that won't be nice; you working somewhere else, I mean. Can I not ask to go with you?"

"Would you really do that for me? No, that's not fair; let's rather discuss a solution jointly."

"What are our options?"

"We are too young to marry or live together, but not too young to be in love. We are what society recognises as young partners because we have declared our love to each other. We have the right to be assigned to work stations jointly."

"That is just swell! I want that for us from now on, do you too?"

"Nothing will give me greater pleasure. I will arrange it."

"Just make sure I stay in the science field for the moment."

"Look, Serge, I just wrote something in the stars with my finger; guess what it is . . ."

"That's easy. I . . . love . . . Serge. Am I right?"

"How did you do that? You write something."

He does.

"Okay, I get it. I . . . love . . . Maddie. Right?"

He laughs. "I'm not saying unless you can catch me."

With that, he runs off, laughing, Maddie in tow. And so they innocently play the hours away. To someone standing far away, they would look like two innocent deer frolicking in the grass.

CHAPTER 22

————•‖═◦❖◦═‖•————

Busy Brumin

The science laboratory is a huge affair—straddling a circumference of four kilometres. On the outside, it is made of soft metal–cum–rock tiles. The inside is lined out with a soft pinkish metallic substance, which is a spaceloy of three metals, one mined on Earth and two on Saturn. It has numerous departments and, like all workplaces, it is manned by humandroids who oversee humans doing service at the laboratory. Each department is centred around a huge, warmly furnished reception hall from which lead all the departmental corridors and rooms. The reception hall also houses the mobile Departmental Control System, which is a humandroid that also functions as the departmental spokesperson. All departmental reception halls are linked to the central reception hall, which houses the Central Laboratory Control, to which all the departmental controls are linked.

Brumin is now working in the two places he requested, the monument and the regeneration department; in other words, his birthplace. The latter consists of ten spacious rooms; four rooms are regeneration wards, three are storage facilities, one is a retirement room for humandroids, one is a general workroom and the last one is a staffroom for humans. He observes that the department underwent some changes since his last 'visit'.

For four months, he learnt about the regeneration process and participated in numerous projects to regenerate skin, tissue and a few organs. At the same time, he has been overseeing the monument.

From day one, he has been a very keen student, pursuing his studies way into the night, and his tutor, Yuri, was extremely impressed with him. His practical work in the laboratory, coupled with the course he followed on biological regeneration, prepared him very well for the task he had set himself.

The department is very quiet at the moment, equipment and facilities merely being maintained in impeccable condition. Brumin is also the only one working in the department at present and his job is to oversee its maintenance. He seldom uses the staffroom, preferring to rest in his birth room, telling Yuri that the room seems to have a calming effect on him.

The graduation was a simple affair. The entire staff and student body associated with the laboratory got together in a huge hall in the complex. After a few speeches, the graduates were called out, received their certificates and applause and that was it. No fancy dress, no hullabaloo, and Brumin was slightly disappointed; at least his family was there and they all made such a big fuss over him.

When they got home, the PAs had arranged a little family party, courtesy of Melanie. The Adams partied late into the evening with the PAs competing to keep them entertained. That night in bed, the next stage of Brumin's plan shifted into gear in his head.

After obtaining his qualification as a regeneration laboratory technician, his activities are no longer supervised. He can call on Yuri at any time for assistance or simply access Departmental Control, and, being an Adam, he is left to his own devices.

Brumin takes another contemplative look at the regeneration caskets and calls Yuri.

"Hello, Brumin."

"Hi, Yuri. I am going to start some experiments; I want to start with trying to regenerate only hair from DNA material."

"What will it be attached to, skin?"

"Yes, will that be okay? May I go ahead?"

"For sure, Brumin. I will send a note to Control, you know this has never been tried; if you can achieve this, it will be a first. Good thinking, Brumin! Will you need any help?"

"Thanks, Yuri, but no, I know how everything works and I want to learn by trial and error; are you okay with that?"

"Yes, Brumin, enjoy your explorations."

"Thanks, my friend."

Poor Yuri, to be tricked like this—he feels almost sorry for his tutor. He kinda likes the willowy Yuri, with his square shoulders, quiet way, clarity of voice and sharp wit. He reminds him of a special uncle. But he has no choice; he cannot proceed without surreptitiousness.

For weeks, Brumin is a very busy young man; his parents and sister hardly ever see him. His nightly escapades make way for work, thinking and studying.

One day, he calls Yuri again and shows him his first result—it is a colourless, soggy piece of skin. Yuri pays close attention to it, but Brumin laughs heartily. "Next time, Yuri, I will call you only once I have been victorious."

Yuri laughs as he departs, blissfully unaware of the graduate's inchoate plan. As soon as Yuri leaves, Brumin starts anew; as soon as he sets up his new experiment, he prepares the regeneration casket next to it for a very peppery dish indeed.

He goes into the store room where the biological specimens from the time capsule are kept. They are stored in five containers that look like ancient Egyptian sarcophagi—if the lights and switches can be overlooked. They give him a feeling of déjà vu and he reads aloud, "Melanie, Pablo, Brumin, Madeleine . . ."

His eyes freeze on the object of his hunt and his voice is suddenly gone—unidentified hair. He goes into a sudden panic as his heart suddenly races with excitement and dread and he has to close his eyes for a minute while he brings himself under control. He takes out the foreign hair that was formerly mixed with his, but separated by the doctor-scientists who had cloned them. He holds it up to admire it—it looks pretty bland. Placing it in the processing unit of the casket, he closes the lid and turns the dial. Having done that, he suffers a momentary flash of rationality as he is suddenly overtaken by an attack of doubt.

"Oh my God . . . What am I doing?"

Another fit of dread takes hold of him as the scope and seriousness of his plans hit home; he cannot move. He holds onto the edge of a shelf and moves slowly to his chair. His mouth is open, he breathes heavily and eyes bob around in their sockets until he closes them and puts his hands over them. He sits like this for a long time, trying to bring under control scores of emotions trying to burst through his chest . . . but then he looks up shakes his head vigorously and his voice comes from a deep place.

"The bloody hell with it!"

Days go by, then weeks.

At the monument, Brumin really has very little to do, as everything is fully automated. Yet he has been quite busy of late, making all sorts of preparations. He needs six secure rooms and a ready supply of food and drink . . . Easy-peasy!

The big day comes on the wings of an insomnious night. Brumin lies in bed, agitated from lack of sleep, thinking, *it is almost time to get up. Now there is no more turning back; this is the day that will change all days; it is the end of my beginning and the beginning of my end. The time for justice has come.*

He gets up slowly, showers a little longer than usual, skips breakfast and leaves for work a little later than usual. After greeting his pilot, he makes the entire journey in silence. Alexandra is by now used to his taciturnity, something she still struggles to fathom.

He walks into his workplace like a zombie; everything looks and feels different today, or is it him? Down a long corridor, he trundles. At last, he gets to the familiar walls of his department, takes off his light jacket and keeps himself busy with his hair experiment, trying his best not to look at the casket next to it. He hums a tune. After about two hours, he goes to the monument. After checking that his preparations are in order, he realises that he needs to arrange food and water; after doing just that, he feels restless and goes home. He sleeps fitfully on his bed and leaves again after dark for the lab, which—like every other workplace—is always open, with people working at all hours, but he discovered that no one else tends to work late on a Wednesday, as it is a huge sports night, nor over weekends.

This time, he is much more focussed and has eyes only for the second casket; he strokes the lid almost lovingly, then pushes a switch. The lid slides away and he injects his patient with the substance that will wake him in exactly fifteen minutes with a sense of tranquillity.

He looks at his handiwork with glee—doesn't it feel great—almost God-like! He created a life—a human being! How innocent he looks! Brumin dresses the young man with old clothes of his father that he brought from home. He waits for him to wake up . . . His patient awakes.

"Hi. My name is Brumin. What is yours?"

"Where am I? Is this a hospital?" He sits up, blinks, blinks, rubs his eyes and lies down again.

"Yes, it is. Do you remember your name?"

He sits up again. "No, I do not know my name. I do not remember anything. You do not look like a doctor. Why is this bed so strange—like a coffin?"

"Okay then, how is Kane? Can I call you Kane until you remember your real name?"

"Okay, but tell me what is going on." He lies down again, feeling very calm.

"Shhhh! We do not have time. Your life is in danger. Soldiers will be here any minute. First, I must take you to a place of safety—there, we will talk."

"Soldiers, danger, why . . . ?" His eyes stretch to their limit. "I'm hungry . . ."

Brumin shows him a packet.

"Listen, we have to get out of here; I will explain later. Eat that on the way. Once outside the building, follow fifteen steps behind me—no one must think we are together. And oh, do not freak out when you see people jumping across the sky or any other funny things, because this is the future—I will tell you about it later, all right . . . Are you listening?"

"Yes, all right, I understand."

Kane's turmoil is hard to bear. People jumping through the sky? Fear, strangeness, discomfort, hunger, anxiety and desperation all roll into a single ball that settles right on top of his heart, which is beating much too fast. Fifteen steps behind him, he said. Who is this guy leading him to God knows where? Why can he not remember his own name? His memory is too sketchy and vague.

Brumin could not do the neural-loading properly without Yuri's help, nor was he interested in doing so. His murderer clone has about fifty percent of his memories—which ones those are, Brumin does not know.

The excitement is almost unbearable for Brumin—he feels he can explode into a thousand bits. The watchword from now on is 'circumspection'. Leaving the building through a back way, he walks in front, chest pushed out, head swollen, and he enjoys Kane's state of exasperation.

There is no one about; things could not have worked out better. Kane is very scared; for him, the terrain is as unfamiliar as the contours of his own face. He looks around for sky-hoppers and freezes when he sees one.

"It's okay," says Brumin. "Let's make haste."

But Kane cannot help himself; he freezes every few minutes to take in the splendid sights against the lights of the night—the pyramid in the distance, the house art displaying mainly images from his own time, the low mountain with its illuminated waterfall not too far away, travellors dashing away, the beautiful greenery and the soft lighting. Suddenly, he comes to a halt again there are no roads!

But never in his wildest imagination could Kane conjure up the sight that stops him in his tracks once again—a building from his time in the midst of all the neoteric . . . Ahead, Brumin is waiting for him, and he runs the few paces to him.

"What in the name of . . . ? Are we in Am-?"

Brumin laughs. "Don't worry, this is only a monument. Be quiet now and follow me inside."

"Inside this place? Wow!"

At last, they are inside. He takes Kane to a huge sparsely furnished room in the west wing.

"This will be your room until we can sort out what to do. As you can see, there is a bed made on the floor. Come on, sit down. We have a lot of catching up to do."

"Can I catch my breath first? I need to absorb everything still; this has been a very busy night . . ."

"Very busy indeed, Kane. Oh, I put some food under this lid earlier, eat first."

"Yes, I am totally hungry . . . a bit grim around the mouth. Hmmm, this looks strange, but good."

Brumin watches as he finishes off the food hungrily, and talks again only when he wipes his hands on the towel provided.

"Now, prepare yourself for the most amazing story you will ever hear. The year is 9 266 . . ."

"What? How can I be here?"

"Shhh . . . Not so loud. The government decided to clone as many primitives—that's what they call you—as they can and use them to test new weapons on. They will all die vicious deaths. You have been cloned. I am a member of the PRAB—People's Resistance Against Brutality; we are working against the government's plan. We have various places of safety around the country for your protection and will integrate you into society later, but at the moment the government has a device that can identify all clones very easily. This place—the Monument of Power—is safe if you do not go out of this room. This building is a monument in honour of what is called The Country of the Brave. It honours the nation that has been the most efficient killers in history. Throughout the day and even during the night, people come in and out on tours. No one comes inside this room, but keep it locked and then take the key out so that I can enter whenever I wish. If anyone comes in here by accident, you must make sure that you are not seen. If you are seen, we cannot help you any longer. I will bring food and water every day because I work in this building.

"And oh yes, if you by chance see me bring other refugees into the building at night, keep your distance. It is better that clones do not know each other."

Brumin enjoys spinning yarn after yarn to keep Kane enthralled and in his power. He is surprised by the amazing tales he spun together so glibly—so he does have an imagination, after all—what do you say now, Mrs. Johnson English teacher? As Kane flicks question after question at Brumin, he does not perceive how the latter appears to be studying every line in his face as if to etch the image in his brain. The almost round face, fat cheeks, stubble on his chin, thin moustache, eyes that have a gleam in them and that are almost too close to each other, and slightly thick lips. Poor Kane. As he listens to Brumin with mouth agape, he feels how his heart is shrinking, shrinking, shrinking.

"Oh, do you like your room?"

"Yes, thanks, man; it is great . . ."

He gets up and walks around the spacious room—the walls are white with paintings on two of them; besides the bed made on a thick carpet, there is a strange antique dressing table, a bookshelf filled with reading material, two big coffee tables with vases filled with roses and three velvety, comfortable chairs. He notices a second door for the first time, and opens it and stands in an exiguous ablution facility.

"My own bathroom! Grand, Brumin, quite grand!"

It has a toilet, shower and wash basin.

Brumin has left and Kane struggles to fall asleep. Whenever he floats away on a cloud, the nastiest monstrosities scare him awake. Men and women with twisted demonic features, armed to the teeth with horrible weapons, searching high and low for clones who all look just like him. So it continues throughout the night.

When he awakes in the morning, he feels like someone who had just run a marathon.

After terrorising his clone with his stories, Brumin sets out for home, pretty chuffed with the coming together of his insidious plan. On the way, he mulls over the face of Kane. The face that was pushed right into his when he was shot in the head. The face that snarled at his sister as she begged for their lives. His face hardens. His body stiffens as his pace quickens. By the time he crawls under the blankets, he is a very angry young man. As he falls asleep, a smile twists the corners of his mouth. His right hand clutches, lifts and stabs, stabs, stabs, while his upper lip pulls back in a snarl . . .

For a whole month, Kane is afraid to leave his room. Then the white walls start to close in on him. It takes two more days for his fears of what lie beyond his door to give way to his urge for freedom. He starts skulking out of his suite late at night, avoiding uncovered windows and lights left on. He does what he can to not be seen by the hidden cameras that Brumin warned him of. Every night, he explores a different section of the monument, unable to access some. His favourite place becomes the egg-shaped office that sits in the eastern corner of the west wing, on the first floor. It is the only place he manages to have fun in his miserable life. He sits at the desk for hours thinking about major events associated with that office that he sketchily remembers at times—his memory no doubt jolted by the various write-ups throughout the building. But he stands for hours at the side of the window, peering at the lawn and the beckoning landscape beyond.

Kane looks at the clock against the wall—23:00! He watches from the window as Brumin crosses the lawn with a visibly nervous refugee about fifteen steps in tow. Kane hastens to his room in case Brumin decides to check up on him. He cannot put his finger on it, but he is a bit scared of the young man with the cold eyes.

What Kane saw was Brumin bringing Kane 6 to 'safety'. Over a period of two months, Brumin had cloned altogether five more Kanes, one at a time, and smuggled them to prepared rooms in either the west or east wings. He ensured that it was impossible for two refugees to accidentally meet up by keeping strategic doors locked. He named each one Kane, and, in his mind, he called them Kane, Kane 2, Kane 3 and so on. He visits them on different nights; sometimes he visits two a night, but he worked out an amazing routine of taking them all food and drink during the day without being seen by uninvited eyes. Every time he raises one from the dead, he feels the same surging climax. How wonderful they look, God's children, *his* children!

Then it was time again to scare them some more. Brumin visits his prisoners one by one, telling them tales of ten refugees who were caught by the police and who subsequently died after technologically advanced weapons were tested on them. Brumin is in his element; never before has he felt so powerful. He has six murderers eating out of the palm of his hand. He gave them life, he sustains them and he will take away their lives at his whim. He is their jury. Guilty! He is their judge. Guilty! Sentencing has been done. Execution is nigh! He leaves them, whistling in the dark.

CHAPTER 23

———◆═:═◆◦○◦◆◦○◦◆═:═◆———

Tracking

Gaston leaves early for a meeting at the Animal Department Services.

An only child, he lives on his own in a cosy bachelor pad, which is smaller than a house, in that it has only two bedrooms and no media room, but a media corner in the lounge. He is in his twenty-fifth year, no special girlfriend, and enjoys flitting from workstation to workstation. He is currently studying to specialise in engineering and spends a lot of time on his hobbies—archaeology and jogging.

He works hard, studies hard and loves socialising with his friends and family. A very easy-going young man, he has a great sense of humour and people love being around him. Women find him very attractive, but he has not yet shown interest in any special one; when asked about it, he says that his mom is the only special woman in his life.

Gaston is very much a typical young man. A chess grandmaster, excellent baseball, table tennis and volley ball player, with well-developed artistic skills, and he has already penned three books.

Since the assembly, his life has been in turmoil. He did not get sick, nor did his mom or dad, though he lost a few friends and acquaintances in the suicidal tide. He feels thankful that no one blames him for what transpired; although he does not blame himself anymore, he has been wishing there was something he could do. Gaston developed some sort of a fetish for the Adam family. Maybe, he thinks, it is an effort to regain his peace of mind.

He communicates a lot with them and is busy developing a digital scrapbook of the family's life and era. He spends a lot of time following all developments around them, including events in the area they live, Spallindaba.

When the animal carcasses were discovered in the Spallindaba Forest, he immediately contacted Animal Services Control requesting that he be allowed to investigate the cause of the deaths of those poor animals. His request was acceded to and, since then, he has been using every available moment to learn about detective work, finding lots of interesting information from the nineteenth to twenty-first centuries. He puts the travellor on auto-pilot, then goes to the luxurious lounge to enjoy the sweeping landscapes from the wide rear and side windows.

It is mid-morning when he alights from the travellor in front of a brownish and glitzy two-storey building—the highest allowed—and the sun is shining brightly. A breeze gently plays through the leaves and refreshes his face; he takes in the fresh and crispy air with relish.

He takes the stairs to the top floor, then enters the boardroom in the Animal Department Services for a briefing. The room is not very big, with a table in the centre and on two wooden-panelled walls two media screens in the on position. Three cabinets surround the room, with a wooden door next to each. His hostess is already waiting for him and, minutes after him, a pretty young woman enters the room and sits next to him.

"Hi, Gaston and Nadz. I am Andrea, the representative of Animal Services Control who will work closely with you throughout the investigation."

"Hi, Andrea! Hi, Nadz!" He waves with a smile.

"Pleased to meet you both, Andrea and Gaston," she says in a fruity, breezy voice that causes Gaston to hold his breath without realising it.

They all shake hands; hers is warm and . . . nice.

"Two days ago, a group of hikers found a decaying carcass of a deer in the Spallindaba Forest. What is disturbing about this find is that the carcass was bloodied.

"Upon an initial investigation by the department, three more carcasses were found, hidden under brushes—each with a piece cut out of it—in locations marked on the map in front of you. That shocking find led to the decision to push the investigation into high gear, which is why you two are now here. Your task is to conduct an in-depth investigation so that the department can understand how this came about and work towards preventing future repetitions. I am assigned to act as your chief resource . . ."

"Thanks, Andrea . . . the best thing now is for us to visit the sites and explore a bit; how far away is Spallindaba Forest from here? What do you think, Gaston?"

"One thousand two hundred and twenty-four kilometres and, as you can see on the map, it is approximately four kilometres by three kilometres and is on the northern fringe of the residential area of the same name, which is divided into five areas."

"I agree with Nadz. I suggest the three of us visit the sites where the carcasses are straight away and look around a bit. What do you think, Gaston?"

"Yes, let's go! We can use my travellor."

The journey takes about fifteen minutes at high speed. The forest is breathtaking. Huge and tall trees mix with bush and brush. Thick clumps of trees are interrupted by clearings of grass and flowers. Fruit hangs from trees everywhere. Creepers with flowers of all shapes and colours curl around trees and hang from others like broken washing lines of old. Here and there, the canopies made by giant trees prevent the sun from reaching the ground.

The carcasses were found in a section of the forest roughly six hundred by four hundred and fifty metres. Andrea clears away the brushes on the first carcass and shines a laser from a finger over it to kill any micro organisms and parasites; they then inspect it together.

"Poor animal! So sorry this had to happen to you, old chum, so sorry." Gaston looks truly mournful. "Neck slit with a sharp object!"

"Oh my gosh! This is heinous! It was done by a human being! And look here, the leg is cut off here! I have never seen or heard of anything like this in all my life!"

They walk from the one dull-eyed carcass to the next and inspect each one, only to find the exact same result. When they reach the last one, Nadz asks Andrea, "Do we have any equipment to scour the terrain?"

"I can do it myself. What are we looking for?"

"Examine the area within a radius of three hundred metres around the carcasses and look for anything that is contrary to the natural state of the environment."

"Nadz, let's sit here and discuss what we found so far. Andrea, will you map everything you find?"

"I will, Gaston . . . see you in a jiffy." She moves away swiftly, with her eyes shining a red laser light that is scouring every millimetre of the terrain.

"This is what it looks like to me, Nadz, someone, or more than one person, did this. The purpose for these killings appears to have been to remove a leg of the animals. What purpose could this serve? I do not wish to speculate at this moment; I will wait to see what Andrea uncovers. What do you think?"

"I agree with you, so let's rest a while until she comes back."

They both sit against a tree. She closes her eyes.

"Tired?"

"A little . . . my friends threw a party for me last night to wish me *bon voyage*, so I hardly slept," she says in that calm, slow, light voice of hers.

Both of them feel a sense of fearful expectation slowly creeping up on them as they wait in solemn silence.

"I'm back." She sits down. "I found sites where four fires have been made. I also found four leg bones and, in addition, I found the body of a pet tiger, which appears to have been killed in a very violent manner. Most of the flesh on the leg bones is removed and

I found teeth marks on two of them. I recorded images of all the sites and bones."

"Is any part of the pet tiger missing?" asks Nadz.

"No."

"Show us the sites where you found these things, please. I would like to look at all the evidence."

"Okay, Gaston, follow me."

After spending a while looking over the evidence and making his own written notes like an old-fashioned PI, despite feeling a little sick in the gut, Gaston suggests they go back to the department to have some lunch, analyse and discuss their findings and work out where to from here.

The first half of the journey back is undertaken in silence, as both are still trying to shake off the terrible foreboding they feel, then Gaston realises he has to do something to get them both out of their trances.

"So tell me about yourself, Nadz; how did you end up in this job?"

"I'm from Cothica and had just finished my service in the archaeology department when I was assigned here by Service Control, and you?"

"Archaeology is one of my hobbies! I live in Pontiac and requested this job when I found out about the deaths. I think I have an obsession with the Adam family; this is an opportunity to be near them."

"May I ask why?"

"Maybe because I discovered the time capsule and blame myself a little bit for what happened after it was opened . . ."

"You found it! Man, I'm in the presence of celebrity! Great going there! You opened up an entirely new world for us, changing ours forever. I think that makes you the greatest man alive!"

"Quit joking. I'm serious . . ."

"I really believe what I'm saying; what happened, happened—it is nobody's fault—you know that, I'm sure. If you did not find the box, someone else would have, maybe centuries later and maybe

Leon G. Caesar

many more people would have died . . . . Do you see where I am going with this?"

"Yeah, I never thought of it like this. I was just a messenger of the universe, in the right place at the right time. I have to accept my lot . . ." The last part, he says quite emphatically. He smiles at her. "Where have you been all my life, Nadz?"

She just laughs softly and he looks at her like he wants to say something.

"What?"

"Nothing." He turns away before she sees him blush.

Just when their minds are cleared of the images and thoughts of death and sorrow, they arrive at their destination.

CHAPTER 24

To Catch a Culprit

T he investigating team worked out that the same person or persons must be responsible for all the killings. They concluded that the legs must have been removed in order to eat the meat. All clues point to the Adam family, for no modern person would be able to eat meat, let alone kill an animal.

How to continue given that it is not allowed to investigate people without their knowledge? Add to that the fact that no person has been investigated for thousands of years.

To respect the rights of everybody, the matter is supposed to be discussed with the family, but the Council of the Realm rejected that possibility because it may be too traumatic. It decided that it would be better for the team to investigate individual members of the family in secret, until they uncover the truth. The investigation will remain secret until the council decides to make it public.

Isn't it just such a sad turn of events that the Adam family must now be under such a terrible cloud? He is alone with his thoughts as he sits in his travellor high up above the Adams' house, keeping watch by means of the travellor's intricate system of cameras. Who is it? Madeleine? Melanie? Pablo? Brumin? Some of them? All of them? He wishes that it is none of them. He wishes that it can all be explained easily. He has been doing this for three days; nothing happened. He is relieved that humandroids are being posted in the forest at night to guard the animals.

Wait a minute, someone just exited the door; the camera lens focuses automatically. It's Madeleine, strolling away . . . He follows her out of sight and out of earshot, with all the lights off. This goes on for fifteen minutes. She walks in the direction of the forest, then she turns away and goes into the park. Who is that coming to meet her? They hug and kiss. False alarm! Better hurry back.

He gets back to his stake-out position and waits.

Madeleine's beloved drops her off at about 2:00. Later, he checks the time—2:45. He yawns. Suddenly, he sees someone slip out of the door—it is definitely Brumin, dressed in a sweat suit. He follows him slowly just as he had followed Madeleine before. Where is he going to so late at night? Gaston brings the travellor to a stop over the House of Primitive Human Brutality as Brumin enters it. This is very strange; he cannot be working so late; maybe he cannot fall asleep? He waits for him to exit the building, which happens roughly an hour later. He walks a while, then runs the rest of the way at a full trot. Gaston follows him home, waits for him to enter the door after catching his breath, then goes to his own temporary accommodation.

He struggles to fall asleep; the question keeps popping up in his mind: what could Brumin have been doing so late at the monument?

Before he falls asleep, he decides to suggest to his two partners that their travellors be fitted with x-ray cameras so that Brumin can be monitored the next time he enters the monument so late. As he drifts off to sleep, images of carcasses, fires and Brumin are edged out by the smiling face of his sweet colleague—he smiles back.

CHAPTER 25

Murder and Vengeance

Brumin had served justice on Kanes 4 and 5 over a period of two weeks, cremating the bodies with the chemical cremator he found in his workplace store, and discarding the remains through the refuse system. The time has come to serve justice on Kane 3.

Brumin has been feeling calm the entire day and goes to bed quite early. After a number of hours of peaceful sleep, he becomes restless. He suddenly sits up in bed, sweating, that dark, heavy, numb feeling spreads from his soul throughout his being. He gets out of bed like he has done so many times before and, with his bag, he leaves for the monument. He takes care that no one sees him. He does not know that Nadz is following him and watching his every move from up high.

Nadz hovers the travellor over the monument. The newly fitted cameras follow Brumin as he walks through the building, up the stairs . . .

As Brumin enters Kane 3's room, the latter is sound asleep; he wakes him up.

"Hi. Shhh. I have to move you to another safe house."

Brumin sits on the floor to the right of Kane's chest.

Kane sits up in his floor bed and rubs his eyes. "Hi, Brumin . . . what time is it?"

"A strange thing happened today—the government sent out a news bulletin explaining that all the clones are dangerous as they are actually murderers. We in PRAB do not think it matters—clones are new people to us and cannot be held responsible for what their genetic donors did in their lives. But do you remember anything about this murderer issue?"

Brumin is watching Kane's face intently.

He is sure he noticed some recognition in the way his jaw suddenly firmed. He looks Brumin straight in the face, then his eyes flash . . .

"You . . . You . . . You are . . ."

He does not finish his thought as the knife glistens in the dim light. His throat is cut with one stroke. As he gurgles on his own blood, paralysed with shock and fear, Brumin pushes his face into his.

"Yes, I am the young boy you and your friends killed in Chelterton, with my sister and mother. I brought you back from Hell to serve justice on you. I am your creator, your jury, judge and executioner. Die, you fuckin' barstard! Go right back to Hell!"

The instrument swishes and swooshes, and Kane's blood gurgles and bubbles. Brumin collapses next to the kicking man, panting, his chest heaving. As he looks through the window, the moon quickly moves behind a cloud . . .

He puts the lifeless body on top of the bed and the cremator next to it. He will apply the cremator tomorrow because it only works on bodies that have lost their heat.

High above, Nadz is paralysed with horror! A voice screams in her head, *he is killing him! Oh my gosh; oh my gosh!*

Everything happened so fast. There was someone there with Brumin, and he killed him! Panic strikes her between the eyes, her heart races and things swirl in front of her. Her stomach heaves and she just manages to get to the bathroom in time.

Back in the cockpit, panic seizes her once more—she hyperventilates, but she manages to press the emergency button. The media screen switches on automatically and a face appears.

"Hello, Nadz. I am Luis. You look pale; is anything the matter?"

The interaction helps her to bring her emotions and breathing under control.

"Luis, I just had a shock like never before in my life . . ." She stops to bring her breathing—that started to run away again—under control again as her heart races anew. "I need something to calm myself. I need to go to the nearest hospital; can you ask Andrea from the Department of Animal Services to bring Gaston to me at the hospital immediately?"

"Sure, go carefully now. A sip of water will do you wonders. I will alert passing vehicles to be on the lookout for you and I will inform the hospital that you are on the way."

"Thanks a lot, bye."

Just then, she faints, which sets off an alarm in Luis' control room. He immediately directs her travellor to the nearest hospital.

She is awoken a minute later by his voice. "Nadz. Nadz, where are you? Nadz . . ."

"I'm here . . . Is that you, Luis? I think I fainted, but I'm okay now. Thanks for waking me. Auto-pilot on; take me to the nearest hospital, please; this is an emergency." She helps herself to some water from the mini bar, then collapses in her seat.

As Brumin walks home along the tree-lined lanes, he plays the scene over and over in his mind. He is fascinated that Kane 3 remembered him! That bastard paid for his crimes. He feels satisfied and smiles as he recalls an old saying: the Lord giveth and the Lord taketh away . . . . His private mirth turns to a sense of panic as he suddenly becomes aware of a multitude of accusing eyes following him, stabbing him. Even the trees are admonishingly bending towards him, shaking their heads slowly . . . He starts to trot and, at that very moment, a breeze comes up and plays through the leaves, and whispers lamentably—

Brumin. Brumin, what have you done?
Brumin. Brumin, why do you run?
Brumin. Brumin, where is your pride?
Brumin. Brumin, there's nowhere to hide.

Away; he must get away, and his legs run as they have never run before until he comes to a halt in a section of the town he had never been in before. After catching his breath, he suddenly stiffens and his eyeballs harden. He turns around and walks determinedly back, back in the direction of the monument.

CHAPTER 26

Change of Track

Gaston and Andrea arrive at the hospital soon after Nadz and find her in her suite; she received treatment for shock and mental trauma and will spend the night.

"Hello, you two."

Her voice is still shaky and Gaston has to restrain himself from putting his arms around her.

"I was witness to something unspeakable, terribly egregious. I cannot bring myself to speak of it. Can you view the recording made by the travellor as a matter of urgency?"

"Nadz, you rest and get well again. Andrea and I will handle this matter until you can join us again. Is that acceptable to you?"

"Will do, Gaston. Thanks a lot. I will be kicked out of the hospital tomorrow, then I will join you again." She squeezes his hand.

Back in the travellor, the two watch the recording in silence. Gaston has to rush to the bathroom as his stomach heaves violently. Andrea pauses the footage until he returns.

"Sorry about that; I now understand why Nadz was quaking in her boots."

They continue watching.

"There he leaves—now why is Nadz staying in one place?"

"She fainted."

"So what do we do now? Call Council Control with our evidence?"

Andrea stops him when he wants to switch the recording off. "Let us watch till the end."

"What is that there, Andrea?" He pauses the recording.

She zooms in and enlarges the periphery of the building. "Someone is coming to the monument."

To their horror of horrors, they see it is Brumin returning! They cannot, they may not allow another murder!

"And look at this, here in this room . . . it is a man standing next to the window!"

"I don't think Nadz saw Brumin go back! This was a while ago already! Let's haste there! You pilot, Andrea, please."

Andrea is already in the pilot seat.

They scour the building with the x-ray camera before landing in front of the door; it took them five minutes to get there, having flown at top speed all the way.

Kane is standing by the window in his favourite room. Never did he dream he would one day be able to set foot in this illustrious office—not even in seven thousand years!

He stands by the window overlooking the lawn when he sees Brumin leaving the premises in the moonlight. He wanted to go to him when he saw him arrive, but something in his manner prevented him. He is still standing at the window when, a while later, Brumin returns. Kane decides to go down and see what he is up to. Once Brumin is inside, Kane follows him without being seen. Brumin unlocks a door, but does not lock it after him. Kane peers around the door post just in time to see another door close; now he makes haste.

He listens at the door to the muffled voices and suddenly he feels guilty because he is spying on the selfless Brumin busy saving souls—including his own. Then he hears a heartrending shriek and he rushes into the room.

"Brumin!"

He stops in his tracks. In the dim light, he sees a man lying on his back, kicking, with blood spurting from his neck. The shock with which he registered that the dying man is his mirror image gives Brumin the advantage with which to kick him to the ground. Within seconds, Brumin has his knee on Kane's chest and his weapon hurtling down when Andrea bursts into the room, her right hand shooting out like the head of a cobra, seizing his wrist in a grip of steel and snatching the weapon with her other hand, with Gaston four minutes behind his fleet-footed assistant.

Kane pushes Brumin off him with vehemence and sits up, looking at Andrea, who is tending to the dying man.

"I'm afraid we are too late," she informs them. "The poor man has deceased."

Gaston looks at the body, then at Kane, then at Brumin, who is breathing heavily.

"Hi, I'm Kane," he introduces himself solemnly, bringing Gaston to his senses.

"Hello, Kane. I am Gaston and this is Andrea. Hello, Brumin; can you two explain to us what has been going on here?"

"There is one more," says Brumin.

"One more what?" Kane is perplexed.

"One more Kane, Kane 2."

You can poke the silence with a stick. Gaston comes to first.

"Take us to him, please Brumin, then you explain everything to us."

Kane pulls him roughly to his feet.

Gaston intervenes, "No, Kane—we must treat Brumin with respect."

Brumin leads the way to Kane 2, who wakes up from the noise they make as they enter his quarters and sits up abruptly.

"What in the . . . ?" His voice trails off as he looks at Kane with a dumb expression on his face.

At last, Kane 2 gets his voice back.

"What in hell is going on here, Brumin?" He gets up and starts to get dressed.

After the introductions, Brumin sombrely tells them the whole story. For the first time, he talks about the day he, his mom and sister were killed. He talks about the difficulties he had adapting to his new life, the nightmares.

He talks of the cloning of his family, how that gave him the idea to clone the Kanes; his revenge on four of the Kanes. Whereas Gaston expected Brumin to be truculent, having been caught red-handed, he turned out to be a truckler.

When Brumin finishes, the Kanes are truly moved by the revelations.

Kane 2's eyes are wet. "I am sorry that you went through such a lot, Brumin, but I did not kill anybody. I am not responsible for what someone else did. I am just a clone, I am a person in my own right. I understand what you did; maybe I would have done the same."

Gaston looks at him in shock.

Kane also apologises to Brumin with a deep emotion of remorse in his voice for the crimes of his genetic donor. Then he does not know what to do. All the fight is out of him, the only thing he feels is sadness—for Brumin, his family, his 'brothers' and himself.

They sit in utter silence for about fifteen minutes, then Brumin speaks. "I'm sorry too. I don't know what got into me—but I so much wanted revenge . . . . It gave purpose to my existence . . ."

"What you did is totally wrong, Brumin," interjects Gaston. "But I am not going to judge you. Did you kill the tiger and the deer?"

Brumin sheepishly admits guilt and does not withhold any information and, after he had so un-bosomed himself, he felt spent, but calm inside.

Gaston goes out of his way to reassure the Kanes that they do not have to worry about anything, that they will be integrated into society as full citizens.

The Kanes cannot keep their eyes off the stunning Andrea.

"You saved my life. I did not thank you yet," says Kane. "Thanks. I noticed you are extremely strong . . ."

She smiles. "It was a privilege to be of service. I am a humandroid—in other words, a robotic creation—attached to the Department of Animal Services. Our department has branches throughout the world and we are responsible for the welfare of all animals on the planet."

"Brumin told us a lot about the way things work nowadays, but I do not anymore know what is true and what is not; can we ask you some questions?" Kane wants to know.

"Of course you may; let me first consult with Gaston about what to do next."

CHAPTER 27

Sticking the Pieces Together

"Gerry . . . Prrrrp, prrrrp. Gerry . . . Prrrrp, prrrp . . ."

PM calls inside his head, with the sudden vibration of his side of the bed waking him. He sits up, suddenly wide awake, looking at Annabelle to see if she is all right, then he looks at the clock—5:30.

"Thank you for waking me, PM. What is the matter?" He whispers, as he does not want to wake his beloved.

"PA asked me to wake you, there is an emergency with regards to the Adam family. Your assistance is required as a matter of urgency. PA is waiting for you in the kitchen."

"Thanks, tell him I'm on my way." He hastily puts on some clothes and slips into his morning slippers.

He finds PA in the kitchen, talking to Gaston via the media unit. "Good morning, everyone."

"Hello, Gerry . . . the travellor is waiting outside. Shall I brief Annabelle and ask her to help me pack some clothes for you?"

"Sure, PA . . . thanks a lot."

Gerry greets the screen again, "Hi, Gaston. I am ready for the briefing." After listening to him for five minutes, he stops him. "Gaston, I am leaving immediately. Let Andrea complete the report on the travellor; that will save me some time."

"Will do, Gerry, and thanks for responding with such speed."

Gerry hastens to the travellor with the travelling bag Annabelle packed for him.

"Hi, Aaron, we are going to the House of Primitive Human Brutality; it is a truly exigent situation, so we need to travel as fast as we can. I will clean and dress so long."

With that, he goes into the bathroom. As soon as Gerry buckles up in his seat, Aaron engages the automatic pilot, says the co-ordinates and address out loud and pushes the speed lever to its maximum. They soar over the ocean and into the rising sun at 4000km per hour.

In flight, Gerry informs Council Control of the macabre developments. Before the flight is over, Control has communicated with all the councillors and important decisions have already been made.

Gerry is at the rendezvous within thirty minutes. Despite their speed, the ride was smooth and enjoyable.

When he enters the room, he takes the situation in with a glance. He greets everybody and looks for a long time at the identical men sitting either side of a hunched-up Brumin, who seems much smaller than he remembers.

He has a few questions for Gaston and Andrea, and listens in disbelief and sadness at their replies, yet his natural leadership qualities come to the fore automatically. First, he must remove as much of the fear he feels in the room as he can, because fear diminishes our humanity. He shakes hands with the two Kanes, introduces himself, welcomes them to their new lives and tells them that they have nothing to worry about—they will be very well looked after by society and they will lead fruitful and meaningful lives like all citizens of the world. He then turns to Brumin.

"Brumin, even though you are responsible for your actions, I believe that society—in particular the Council of the Realm— is partly responsible for everything that transpired. Your urge for vengeance came from somewhere and we did not detect or treat it. The council will decide where we—and I mean the entire society—go to from here. I am very sorry that the society we brought you into allowed this situation to occur. I want you to know that the council will do what is in the best interest of everybody, including what is in your best interest. The Council of the Realm already agreed to convene an Extraordinary Conference to deal with the situation. Council Control has already taken steps to place your PA on safety mode until the conference maps out the way ahead. An Extraordinary Conference includes delegates from all the regions of all the continents, and it supersedes the Council of the Realm. When your PA is placed on safety mode, it will ensure that you do not hurt yourself or any other living creature. It will also follow you wherever you go, just until the situation is sorted out."

Gerry's calmness reassures everyone; little do they know that he actually feels like a cat on hot bricks.

Gerry receives a communication from Council Control. Wheels have been set in motion; a house has been arranged for the two Kanes to stay in temporarily, with a PA for each of them. A team of two councillors, two doctor-scientists, and a psychologist are on the way to pick them up and to induct them into their new lives. The PAs will bring them up to speed on developments over the past seven thousand years.

Gerry takes Brumin home in his travellor. As they leave, Brumin feels the urge to turn around and looks through the back window. He takes a long and hard look at the majestic white monument.

During the journey, Brumin is very quiet, causing Gerry to feel absolutely sorry for him.

"Brumin, your parents and sister have to be informed of everything that happened. I have to inform them, but it may be better if you speak to them first. What do you prefer?"

"I will tell them, Gerry, in the morning."

"Good, I will then come over in the evening to chat with them about it and to see how they are handling the situation.

Can you arrange for your PA to call me to give me a time for the get-together?"

"Sure, Gerry, and Gerry, I'm sorry about everything."

"I know you are, son, I am too." He puts a comforting hand on the youngster.

Brumin's PA meets him at the door. Until further notice, his PA will henceforth always accompany him wherever he goes, and will always know exactly where he is and what he is doing.

CHAPTER 28

———— •┅╬┅◈◖◗◈┅╬┅• ————

The Mark of Kane

K ane and Kane 2 live about fifty kilometres from the Adams in a similar, but smaller, house. They settled in quite easily and enjoy the comforts of their new lives. Their sessions with the doctor-scientists and the psychologist did a lot to help them come to terms with their past.

The councillors who brought them to their new house are Fatima and Yevgeni, both of whom became the committee to oversee their adaptation.

Their PAs, Sybil and Nandi, were on safety mode for one week only. In one of the first sessions with the Kanes, Fatima and Yevgeni told them that they did not have to keep the names given to them by Brumin, but that they may choose any names they prefer. Kane is now Jamie Kane and Kane 2 is now Jerome Kane. Surprisingly, they both decided to keep the name Kane; they say it is to remind them of the crimes that their gene donor committed.

The Council of the Realm is quite pleased with their adaptation.

Jamie and Jerome are like twin brothers; they do lots of things together and talk about all sorts of things. One morning, Jamie finds Jerome sitting in the kitchen, looking very upset.

"What's up, brother? You look terrible."

"Everything came back to me . . . last night . . . I remembered how I, we, murdered the poor Adams."

"Hold it right there, Jerome! We did nothing, do not blame yourself for what that idiot did whose genes we carry." He comes closer to him and holds him by the shoulders.

"Here, I have learnt to look at the facts. We are innocent; we are on this Earth only for a few months. we know not the old, primitive world. Look around you; this is our world. We are modern people."

"I know, Jamie. It is just that the memories are so powerful . . ."

"Yes, they will be powerful, but the facts are more powerful; those memories are like a movie planted in your head. Do not go the same road that Brumin went; if you don't shake off this nonsense, I will ask Sybil to knock you on the head! Agreed?"

At this, Jerome bursts out laughing. "No, thanks. You are right. Don't worry about me; I am fine, really, but I do think it would help me if I can become friends with Brumin and his whole family."

"Not a bad idea; let's arrange our first visit."

CHAPTER 29

·:═◄●●○●►═:·

A Mother's Heart

The Adams are all sitting in the living room. Melanie remembers the events of the morning. Brumin was late for breakfast; she called him on her wrist communicator and still joked with him, "Hey, young man, sleeping late, we are eating already. You coming?"

"Morning, Mom. In a few minutes . . . you go ahead, but everyone must wait for me, as I have something very important to tell you. I love you, Mom."

She was too stunned to reply. When last did she hear any words of affection from him? His tone of voice bothered her; nay, it scared her.

"Brumin is on his way; he wants to talk to us about something important."

"Aw, Mom, Serge is waiting for me . . ."

"Come on, Mads . . ." Her father sounds impatient. "How often does Brumin want to talk to us? This is an event worth making Serge wait to see your pretty face."

How right he was.

"I guess you're right, Dad. He better come quickly." She barked into her wrist communicator, "Come now, sleepy head! I have an appointment with someone very special."

The pained, solemn look in Brumin's eyes brings a gasp to her lips.

"Mom, Dad, Madeleine, I did something terrible; I am so sorry . . ." He slumps into a chair, face in his hands for a few minutes while he struggles to get his breathing under control. When he lifts his face, his eyes are wet and his cheeks are smudged.

Melanie nearly has kittens. "Brumin!"

As she gets up to go to him, Pablo pulls her by the sleeve, slowly shaking his head at her. She sits down, waiting silently.

No one speaks again until Brumin has finished telling his awful tale. First, there is a poignant silence as they look at their brother and son, who is coming apart at the seams. While Melanie listened to his confession, she became very, very calm, her breathing slowed down and so did her heart rate. Her heart breaks with his as she looks at the pathetic heap sobbing with his face on his arms. Every fibre in her body wants to react in panic, her son, her wonderful son! But she sits still and forces every emotion to her brain. Her family was prematurely destroyed once; it will not happen again.

Madeleine is the first to talk. "That is awful, Brumin . . . I don't know what to say . . . Dad, Mom, what is going to happen to Brumin now?"

"Son . . ." Pablo starts. "It is difficult to know what to say. I know it does not help to cry over spilt milk, but I think you must be punished. Murder is a capital crime. When Gerry comes, I will tell him that justice must be done. But I think I speak for the whole family if I say that, no matter what happens, we will all support you through it. We can all see that you have remorse for what you have done, and, for the life of me, I do not know to what extent the regeneration process caused you to act the way you did. On the other hand, you are an adult and fully responsible for your actions . . ." He throws his hands in the air.

"No, Pablo, I do not think you should do that. He is clearly sorry for what he has done and, as you say, there are certainly mitigating circumstances. Let us rather ask the council to be lenient with him, give him another chance."

"No, Mom, Dad is right! I do not know if I can ever get over this, because I feel that our entire family is mixed up in this, but punishment will definitely help me come to terms with everything. What will Serge say about this?"

The family has a lengthy discussion about this, but Melanie does not budge from her position.

In her heart, he is still her little boy and she wants to protect him.

"Brumin . . ."

"Yes, Mom?"

"The neighbour's dog, tell us about that . . ."

"It was me . . . I killed it . . ." His face falls onto his arms again. "I'm sorry . . ."

"Why, Brumin, why did you kill that dog?"

He sits up again. "I don't know, Dad . . . It started when I was small, first crickets and spiders, then frogs . . . birds . . . later a chicken . . . and then the dog . . . I don't know why; I guess the old Brumin was pretty messed up; now I'm doing worse things."

After the family discussion, Melanie feels languid; she gets back into bed and asks her PA to inform her work that she will be absent for the rest of the week. She does not even want to speak to Pablo and sulks like this for a couple of hours. Later, she goes to sit in the garden, trying to clear her mind; she then calls her PA and chats to him for a long time about her emotional turmoil. By the time Gerry arrives for dinner, she is thinking clearly, she is resolute.

He tries his best to keep a stiff upper lip. "I am glad that Brumin informed you all of what had transpired. It took a lot of courage of him to tell you himself. Before I go any further, do you have any questions for me?"

Pablo is the first to reply. "We are all very sorry about this, Gerry, and please convey our sense of anguish to the council. We would obviously like to know what will happen now. For my part,

I believe that Brumin should be punished; only then will justice be served."

"I agree . . ."

The other Adams are surprised at Melanie's change of heart.

She continues, "I believe that the regeneration process is greatly to blame, but he is an adult and responsible for his actions; only punishment will help to right the wrongs."

"What idea do you have of punishment, Melanie, Pablo?"

"I was thinking of a prison term," says Pablo.

Melanie concurs.

"Prisons were abolished thousands of years ago, as monstrosities that dehumanise all of us. Our approach to wrong-doing is to put the blame where it belongs, to find a just way forward and to rehabilitate where needed. Justice has many times just been another word for revenge."

"But what about the victims?" Madeleine wants to know. "It is fine to be compassionate towards the criminal, but who is going to speak for them?"

"Madeleine, you have a good point, but answer me this. I read of a case in your era in which a man killed a woman very brutally and was killed by the state as a result. This man was pure evil and, when I dug deeper into his life, I discovered that he grew up in an abusive and unloving home. He was abused and neglected from before he could even walk. He was raped by his own uncle at the age of ten. He grew up witnessing his father continually abusing his mother. He left home at the age of fourteen and started fending for himself. At every job he found from there on, he was further abused in the form of being underpaid and over worked. He stopped working after six years and started living off the proceeds of crime. Then he started hurting people, killing, raping, assaulting. He is on record as saying that he felt absolutely nothing when he hurt other human beings and that he did not know how to feel remorse. He said that he also did not care whether he lived or died. Now, I ask you, do you think that punishing him solved anything? Was the perpetrator not himself a victim?"

Madeleine does not answer; she just lowers her head on her hands.

Gerry continues, "Punishing did nothing for the victim, but certainly gave the living a sense of revenge. Punishing this unfortunate soul was a knee-jerk reaction where society hurt the individual whose crimes it created in the first place. We have learnt from the past. In the matter before us, we need to understand what happened and why, how to ensure no one affected, including Brumin, is disadvantaged and, most importantly, how to ensure society goes forward from this situation with dignity. And the victims, we never forget them; their only justice can be a world free of abuse and violence."

The discussion continues late into the night and, in the end, Melanie and Madeleine accept what Gerry said, though hesitantly, but Pablo does not budge. Finally, Gerry invites Pablo to forward his point of view to the Extraordinary Conference.

"I will do so, Gerry, but where, at court?"

"What is that?"

Madeleine explains the functions of courts as best she can.

"We do not have courts, or judges or lawyers. There will be no prosecution and no defence; there will rather be a pooling of minds and compassion to search for the truth, the whole truth. In the end, the society as a whole will decide on the best way to deal with the situation."

"Can I say something?" a sheepish Brumin wants to know. He continues when Gerry nods. "I would like to be punished . . . please . . . to somehow make amends."

"Why don't you also submit your views to the Extraordinary Conference?"

"All right, I would love to. Thanks, Gerry."

CHAPTER 30

———— •—::—◆◆◇◆◇◆◇◆◇◆——::—• ————

Please Let Me Pay!

T wo days after Gerry's visit, two members of the council and two psychologists spent one entire week with Pablo and Melanie in a holiday villa, helping them deal with the developments . . . . Brumin wanted to stay home to work on his submission to the conference and Madeleine said that she did not need support; Serge was helping her through it all.

Madeleine seems to have moved on quite easily; she spends even more time than usual with Serge. Once, while he was sitting in her embrace, she admitted that, if it was not for his love and support, she would have been a real mess. He just smiled as he turned his head up to look into her eyes.

Brumin uses the week to reflect and to draft his submission. He writes about the night his family was slain, about how he felt while they were being terrorised, how his first memory thereafter was of that night, how his leg still seems to throb, and how terrible he feels about what he did. He writes about the need for justice for the victims, and about his need to pay for his crimes.

He mulls over his words, then he is gripped by a sense of terror. *What if they do not punish me; how will I be able to get over this?*

He ends his document by renewing his plea for a prison sentence, adding that, if this is not done, he should be excommunicated to a station on another planet until his life is over. He changes the title to 'Please Let Me Pay for My Crimes!'

After submitting his document to Gerry, he researches the various locations beyond the Earth's frontiers.

CHAPTER 31

❖─❖❖═❖❖○❁○❖═❖❖─❖

Crime, Revenge, Crime, Punishment

The Extraordinary Conference is quite a huge affair. All the thousands of delegates received preparation reports a week in advance.

The conferees divide into twenty commissions, each of which deliberates a set of points developed by Council Control as a guideline. A commission may add or delete points by majority vote. Each commission is facilitated by a pedagogue, a humandroid whose function is to chair deliberations, guide discussions, serve as the information source and report back to the plenary session. One commission deliberates the reports submitted separately by Pablo and Brumin.

The pedagogues report back by downloading their reports directly to Conference Control, which repackages them into a single report for all delegates, who get one day to study it. When the conference reconvenes, the report is debated and voted on. Conference Control analyses the votes, collates the majority decisions under clear headings—listing the percentage of delegates who voted in favour and tabulating minority decisions in similar fashion, printing the conference report and also posting it on the communication network for the public's response.

After the cut-off time for public responses has arrived, Conference Control analyses all responses and makes a few changes in terms of standard conference protocols. All amendments are clearly indicated in the report, as well as the number of people who supported them, and a final report is issued in multimedia format, as well as in print.

Pablo and Melanie sit in the media room, studying the report together. Madeleine is going over it with Serge at his house. Brumin reads it in his room.

Pablo reads the following sections of the report over and over . . .

"Full responsibility for the murders lies with society— today and before. As acts of vengeance, the murders were reactions to severely traumatic deeds and it filled a psychological need, however twisted. When Brumin was regenerated, there were slumbering in his subconscious the seeds that would flower into unstoppable urges for sadism and revenge. As far as the viciousness with which his revenge was fulfilled is concerned, that is a product of the society that he grew up in. The failing of the Council of the Realm is that, when the Adam family was regenerated, it did not keep in mind the possibility of such factors. But the council cannot be fully blamed for this shortcoming, as it reacted to an unprecedented crisis and it was itself a victim of this crisis. What then of Council Control's role in this catastrophe? Society never blames its tools, for they are creations of people and are controlled by citizens.

Society needs to apologise to Brumin and his family for the suffering they went through while in our care. A way needs to be found in which the psychological scars arising from the murders of the family and from the numbing and soul-destroying traits of the old society can be quantified and reversed.

Concerning the four murdered regenerated humans, there is no way that their deaths can be undone; they are the first people to be murdered in over five thousand years. A special monument will be erected in their honour.

Regarding Jamie and Jerome, each is already being fully integrated into society.

The House of Primitive Human Brutality definitely played a role in bringing out Brumin's murderous plans. It is no coincidence that Brumin got the idea of revenge when he was lying on the lawn outside the monument and it is no coincidence that the murders were committed inside it. Society did not even consider that such a dark and sombre monument could have a negative effect on the people we brought back from its time. We still need a monument, but we need to replace the building with a structure that conjures up images of beauty and humanity. When we built the monument, we built a monster that continued its killing spree.

The way things are done needs to be changed. Society now includes people from a time when everyone was bombarded on a daily basis with images of physical, emotional and psychological brutality. A time when the majority of people did not have adequate food, housing or clothes. A time when humanity was ruled not by people who wanted to lead, but by people who protected and maintained the wealth and privileges of a select few. These rulers were mostly greedy and power-hungry people who would generally stop at little in their pursuit of wealth and power for their social class. Whatever we do from here on, we need to be most sensitive and consider how it could affect our new citizens.

As for Brumin and his family, a support structure will be set up as a matter of urgency that will deal with their treatment. Brumin is not to be held responsible for what he did because he is a victim too; he needs love and the necessary support to overcome the deep-seated causes that led him on his killing spree. He will be allocated a bachelor pad—close to his family home—as he is old enough to live on his own. His PA will remain on safe mode until his support structure decides otherwise, which will include his doctor-scientist and two psychologists—one human and one humandroid. They will work intensively with him for as long as it takes. Once they believe that Brumin has fully or adequately recovered from the causes of his actions, he will be allowed to lead a normal life once again. Now, his only responsibility is to get well.

The report calls for a balanced view of what transpired. It must not be forgotten that something positive, something good came out of this episode—two people were regenerated and are now part of our society. Any birth or rebirth is always treasured."

"Pablo, you must admit that what they came up with is much better than prison . . ."

"Mel, yes, and I am glad that not one person agreed with me or with Brumin. You know what, I realise that, with all this love and support, Brumin will most probably actually come right again. For our part, we must also just give him all the love and support we can muster; no more blame."

"I think so too. I learnt a lot from this process. I feel as if I have at last made the shift from the past to the present. Do you get what I'm saying?"

"Yes, very much . . . I feel the same, humbled in a way. I want to call Gerry to tell him that I am happy with the outcome and that I would like the whole world to know!"

"You are beginning to sound more and more like a modern! Don't forget to tell him that we both learnt a lot from the experience, and thank him again for me."

"Another thing, I have had enough of doom and gloom feelings. I want to shake them off. Let's have some fun!"

"I like your thinking, where are we going?"

"Who said anything about going anywhere?"

Their laughter bursts the cloud that has been hanging over their house for weeks.

CHAPTER 32

Bridging Millennia

I n the past two months, Brumin has had a lot of time to think, yet he has been quite busy with his treatment sessions. He was freed from his service obligations, as his treatment is quite intense, and he decided to do his best to overcome his malaise and has been making a lot of progress; however, he cannot shake off his feelings of guilt and sadness.

During this time, Boris has been his close friend and confidante. Always listening patiently, always reassuring.

Various councillors had been popping in to visit him and encourage him. His parents visited a number of times and were always supportive. He looks forward to their visits because he now sees them in a totally new light. Madeleine and Serge also came over a few times and he has grown quite fond of Serge.

It is early evening. Boris is busy somewhere at the back. Brumin responds to the door chime as someone enters.

He stops in his tracks as a dazzling, vivacious young woman appears in front of him.

"Hello, Brumin. I'm Noz'bele I would like to steal you for a while."

He grabs her proffered hand in a daze; he greets her, but no sound emerges. She smiles as she waits patiently.

"Hel-lo."

She keeps his hand and simply leads him out, chatting all the while; they do not notice Boris following closely behind.

"My friends and I are having a get-together and we would like you to join us, it's not far from here. Sorry, I did not give you a chance to say no." She laughs and starts swinging their hands to and fro.

"It's okay . . . I would love that."

He lies through his teeth. Luckily, she talks a lot, which allows him to catch his breath. He feels disappointed when she drops his hand.

He likes the get-together, even with Boris chaperoning him. They are all roughly the same age. They quaff wine, enjoy snacks, entertain each other with songs, poetry recitals, skits, talk about their work and studies, and just enjoy each other's company. And, of course, the main topic of all the performances is *Sylvia's Mother*! By now, Brumin has come to accept this as a fact, waiting patiently for the Sylvia fad to pass. Everyone makes him feel comfortable. No one speaks of his situation. All night, Noz'bele stays close to him, making sure he is all right. Every now and then, she flashes him a broad, reassuring smile. The atmosphere and company gives him a feeling he does not remember—total happiness, and, as another smile is flashed in his direction, he can contain himself no longer. He climbs onto the couch that doubled up that night as a side-stage, and, with no inhibition, he belts out *Sylvia's Mother*, to everybody's delight.

"Brumin, you're a fantastic singer; no one knew that about you."

He looks into her face and smiles as she starts dancing with him.

"And you're a good dancer too; I'm impressed."

He just laughs. "Noz'bele, do you live here?"

"Yes, I live on my own; why, do you want to come visit me?" she teases.

"Yes, would you mind?"

"I will not mind one bit. I would actually like it."

And so starts the most important relationship in his adult life.

When it is time to go home, Noz'bele walks with them, saying, as she brought him, it is only fair that she returns him to his abode. Boris waits for him just inside the door as he and Noz'bele chat for hours on the lawn.

Later, he lies awake, mulling over her every feature. She is slightly taller than him. Her soft, smooth, deep brown skin. Her strong jaw. High cheek bones. Big, brown, almond-shaped eyes. Full lips. Straight shoulders. Upright walk. Dazzling smile. Firmness of character. Open and joyous personality. He falls into a blissful sleep with her aura all around him.

They fall head over heels in love. With Boris in tow, she takes him on numerous outings to show him her favourite places in the world, and she has a couple of those on every continent and a few on some islands. She listens when he talks about his feelings of guilt and sadness; she never says anything, just hugs and kisses him.

He marvels at how neither she nor any of her friends, who are now his friends as well, criticise or judge him for what he did. They have clearly placed his crimes firmly in the past and are focussing on the here and now.

To show his appreciation for his new friends, he surprises them with a new song at every one of their get-togethers. Noz'bele told him that everyone learns to sing, but a voice like his is a special gift from nature.

CHAPTER 33

• ╫═◆◐○◑◆═╫ •

Soaring Hearts

Egbert feels disappointed that he did not detect Brumin's downward mental spiral. He knows he is unfair towards himself, for no one would have been able to, but this feeling spurs him on to at least perform better in the process of healing. He is the co-ordinator of the Brumin Therapy Support Structure. He will not rest until Brumin has been given a clean bill of health.

The others on the Support Structure agree with him; Brumin has made amazing progress, but if he cannot shake off his feelings of guilt and sorrow, he will not be able to live a free life. He knows that time alone will not be sufficient; a powerful intervention is needed. He suffered many sleepless nights wracking his brain, doing research, until he discovered the solution by accident. Now he needs to persuade his colleagues. They are already waiting for him in their allocated office at the Medical-Science Academy.

After the greetings, he gives a lengthy presentation. There was absolutely no discussion; everyone concurred: the human spirit therapy that was used only once before—and with startling success—four thousand years ago, is the answer.

Their recommendation and the presentation had been forwarded to Council Control; the council quickly approved it and put the process in motion.

Now, the time has come. Boris sits with an anxious Brumin in the living room, with the media screen extended to ceiling height. Brumin was informed of the human spirit therapy and his role is that he has to watch the proceedings on the media screen with Boris. At exactly 15:00, all people come out of their houses and work places, switch their wrist-communicators on a specially prepared frequency and grab a hand of the two persons nearest to them. People do this across all continents. Billions of people holding hands at the same time, in the light of the sun, under the light of the moon or simply under the stars. Everyone looks up in concentrated meditation, sending messages to Brumin. The images are brought onto the screen from all over the world. The messages stream down the side, expressing love and support for him, calling on him to put the past behind him, imploring him to embrace life with love and freedom in his heart, telling him that he must not blame himself for what happened as he is himself a victim of circumstance; on and on, the messages go.

He looks at the millions of people standing in the dark, looking to the sky with his name on their minds. Images from all around the world continue to stream slowly across the screen. He sees Gerry, Gaston, and Noz'bele. Beautiful, innocent Noz'bele, with her eyes closed tightly; he sees her lips move. 'Brumin, I love you . . . Brumin, I love you . . . '.

He sees his family; he sees the Kanes. He looks and looks, strangers, millions of strangers thinking of him, Brumin, the young man who had killed so many . . .

He turns away from Boris, puts his face into the couch and weeps, and weeps. The anguish, the sadness, the guilt, pours out of him until there is nothing left. Deep within his breast and his mind, something stirs, something he never felt before; it seems to stand up, dust itself off, stretch its arms out and grow and grow until there is space for nothing else, then he falls into a deep sleep.

He finds himself standing on a cloud, drifting off, higher and higher, until he comes to a huge door that swings open to let him enter. Inside, there is a huge, beautiful, cool lake with crystal-clear water that moves slightly in motion with the light breeze. He cannot resist the power of the water and he jumps in and swims in the freshest water that had ever touched his skin. He is joined by dolphins and penguins that play gaily with him. He loses track of time. After a long while, he gets tired and lies down under the soft sun to rest a while. As the sun warms his body, he closes his eyes; he feels a new oneness, a oneness of heart, mind and soul; a oneness of human, animal, plant, water, sun, earth and wind.

He has found his place in the universe; he is not just a speck in contrast to all eternity; nay, he is a very important part of it all. He feels simply wonderful, beautiful. He feels free.

He comes to as he feels a hand gently stroking his hair, bringing him energy, love and more peace. Noz'bele, sweet Noz'bele. He turns around, adjusts his position, puts his head on her lap and his arms around her waist and falls asleep again. If one can ever imagine a sleep of love, that was exactly what Brumin experienced; he felt wrapped in a blanket of warmth that was filled with soft, soothing, pleasant whispers and touches. In the morning, he awakes on the couch with his face in Noz'bele's neck, wrapped in her arms.

CHAPTER 34

:·❖═◈◆◈═❖·:·

Hope

Three months have come and gone. The Adam house is abuzz with preparations for a gathering. The door chime goes off as someone enters.

"Hello, Brumin! Hello, Boris! Come in; come in!"

"Hello, Mum."

He gives her a peck on the cheek. The chime goes off again and Melanie meets the two Kanes as they enter. After greeting, she takes them to the lounge where everyone else is waiting.

The Kanes, now Jamie and Jerome, requested the meeting.

Everyone awaited the meeting with trepidation. Yet, it was quite an easy and enjoyable occasion. All the Adams appear to be over the past and no one held any ill feelings towards Jamie and Jerome. After all, they are not really the person who participated in the murders by their genetic original.

They enjoyed a sumptuous meal, quaffed all sorts of pleasant drinks and really had some nice conversations. After Jerome and Jamie expressed their regret at what happened in the past and asked to be friends with everyone, the conversation never again goes back to the wiping out of the family. They do talk a lot about the past, but more to compare with the present. They talk a lot about the way things are today and the way things are done.

"Brumin, if it was not for you, the two of us would not have been alive today. We would have missed all this. On behalf of both of us, we thank you from the bottom of our hearts. We will always be grateful to you."

"Thanks, do you work yet?"

"Both of us just started recently, Brumin. I work at the lunar support department. Jerome can speak for himself."

"I am not sure yet what happens on the moon, so what do you do?"

"Madeleine, there is a base on the moon for people from our department who visit from time to time, but there are also holiday houses for people—they are quite popular. The main activity on the moon is mining and processing of all sorts of minerals, gold being one of them, but a couple of metals too that are not found on Earth. The entire operation is done by humandroids. I found out that there are similar colonies on many other planets and moons and they are all staffed by humandroids."

"Fascinating, isn't it? There is so much to find out and so much to learn, and you Jerome?"

"I decided to move from work to work like most citizens do. Currently, I am doing farming. I quite enjoy it, but compared to the farming technology today, what we did in our time was totally primitive! And what about you, where do you all work?"

And so the conversation carries on for hours and hours. It seems the old saying, 'the more the merrier', is absolutely true, for everyone present feels completely at home.

The visitors leave quite late that night. Brumin pilots his own travellor with Boris in the passenger seat.

He stops at the site where the now-infamous monument used to be. Not a sign of it remains. In its place prances a building shaped like a hand, giving the old peace sign. The building is surrounded by huge lawns and flower beds.

Brumin throws himself down on one of the lawns, and looks at the moon and the stars, with Boris watching him from the travellor.

He thinks about the recent past and is thankful that he has been on his own. Since his human spirit therapy session, he has stopped crying. He feels whole, empowered. He knows a peace he never knew before.

He must find a way to thank this unique society for everything it has done for him, for treating him with dignity and respect regardless of his atrocities—and yes, treating him with love and understanding. It must be something big. While trying to come up with something big enough, he falls asleep under the twinkling stars, but not before he winks at the moon that winks right back at him.

PRELUDE

Brumin cannot know that his opportunity will soon beckon as, light years away, a fundamental stirring is taking place in an unknown and vicious world, unleashing an avalanche of deadly energy—faster than the speed of light—in the direction of . . . Earth.

Brumin. Brumin.

Will you have the fortitude, when the time is nigh, to show your gratitude?